Penguin Books

**SONGS OF THE IMMORTALS:**
**AN ANTHOLOGY OF CLASSICAL CHINESE POETRY**

Xu Yuan Zhong, born at Nanchang in China in 1921, obtained his B. A. from National Southwest Associated University in 1943 and his Diploma of Literary Studies from the University of Paris in 1950. He served as an interpreter in the American Volunteer Group during the Second World War and visited Europe after the war. He is professor of world literature at Peking University.

Among his many publications in English are *On Chinese Verse in English Rhyme, Gems of Classical Chinese Poetry in Various English Translations, 150 Tang Poems,* and *300 Tang Poems — A New Translation.* He has also translated 100 Tang and Song lyrical poems into French as well as translating some of the world's masterpieces into Chinese. These include Stendhal's *Le Rouge et le Noir* and Flaubert's *Madame Bovary*.

He is the author of *Art of Translation,* in which he puts forward the principle that a translated verse should not only be faithful but also beautiful, as beautiful as the original in sense, in sound and in form, and he puts his theory into practice in this book.

# SONGS OF THE IMMORTALS

## AN ANTHOLOGY OF CLASSICAL CHINESE POETRY

*Translated and versified by*

XU YUAN ZHONG

Penguin Books in association with New World Press

PENGUIN BOOKS

Published by the Penguin Group
Penguin Books Ltd, 27 Wrights Lane, London W8 5TZ,
England
Penguin Books USA Inc., 375 Hudson Street, New York, New
York 10014, USA
Penguin Books Australia Ltd, Ringwood, Victoria, Australia
Penguin Books Canada Ltd, 10 Alcorn Avenue, Toronto,
Ontario, Canada M4V 3B2
Penguin Books (NZ) Ltd, 182-190 Wairau Road, Auckland 10,
New Zealand

Penguin Books Ltd, Registered Offices: Harmondsworth,
Middlesex, England

First published in the People's Republic of China by New
World Press, Beijing, 1994
Published in Penguin Books 1994

To Peking University,
where I was a student of foreign languages
fifty years ago
and where I am a professor of world literature now.

X. Y. Z.

# CONTENTS

## Tang Dynasty (618-907)

## Song Dynasty (960-1279)

## Yuan Dynasty (1271-1368)

## Ming Dynasty (1368-1644)

## Qing Dynasty (1644-1911)

# INTRODUCTION

## I

"Chinese literature," according to John Turner in his *Golden Treasury of Chinese Poetry*, "is the high artistic peak of the most literary, the most artistic, the longest-established civilization that exists." The earliest anthology of Chinese literature is *The Book of Poetry*, consisting of 305 poems and compiled in the sixth century B.C. It is divided into three main sections: 160 songs, 105 odes, and 40 hymns. The songs are folk songs collected by royal musicians from fifteen feudal states that clustered along the Yellow River; the odes are ceremonial or festive songs composed by official diviners and historians and used before going to war and hunting; the hymns are songs of praise and advice to the ruler, written by officials and used as part of ancestral sacrifices and feasts during the Western Zhou period from the eleventh to the seventh centuries B.C.

The poems centre on daily activities. We see people farming and hunting (*Hunting*), gathering food and courting (*A Fair Maiden*), performing sacrifices and going off to war *(Comradeship)*. Poems about love and marriage form the bulk of the folk songs, presenting the sadness and joy of lovers' partings and reunions, as well as the relative freedom of love in those days for ordinary people (*The Quiet Maiden*). Many of these poems are light-hearted in tone, but others complain of unhappy love affairs or marriages (*A Faithless Man*), misrule or the hardships of soldiering (*Homecoming After War*). The happier songs tend to express feelings directly while the unhappy singer often turns to metaphors. For example, the poet vents his indignation against injustice on earth by enumerating the stars in heaven which do not live up to their fine names:

> In southern sky appears a Winnowing Fan,
> Alas! it can't be used to sift the grain;
> In northern sky a Dipper, which man,
> Alas! would use to ladle wine in vain.

The poem's depth of feeling and unusual artistic technique are remarkable for the Western Zhou period.

Structurally, each line of these poems is made up of four characters (*Homecoming After War*), though lines of other lengths occur at times. The lines are arranged in stanzas, usually of four lines each (*The Cock Is Crowing*). Rhyme is used at the end of the even-numbered lines. Alliteration, assonance, and inner rhyme are also used. Many songs employ repetitions (*My Man's Away*) and refrains, others start a stanza by evoking an image quite apart from the central theme (*The Fruits from Mume Tree Fall*), a device called "evocation" or "association." Conciseness is also a characteristic of the earliest Chinese poetry.

As *The Book of Poetry* was numbered among the Five Confucian Classics, it has had considerable influence because of its use as a basic text in traditional Chinese education.

## II

If *The Book of Poetry* is the earliest anthology of realistic songs composed by the northern people, *The Verse of Chu* may be said to be the earliest collection of romantic poems written by a southern intellectual, Qu Yuan (340-278 B.C.). During Qu Yuan's life, northern realism met southern romanticism. Qu Yuan's blending of the two made him the greatest lyrical poet in the period of the Warring States (475-221 B.C.). His best-known work is his autobiographic long poem *Sorrow After Departure*, which depicts his grief at being estranged from the undiscerning King of Chu. He refers to the king as "Fair One" and "Godly One," and compares his own longing for a discerning king to the quest for an ideal mate. Thus he established in classical Chinese poetry the tradition of using beauty to symbolize the sovereign and fragrant plants to represent loyal ministers and subjects. He writes:

> I did not grieve to see sweet blossoms die away,
> Grieved rather that amid weeds they did decay.

His love for the ideal is so deep that he says:

> Long, long the way, I know not which to go.
> I'd seek my heart's desire both high and low.

He could not bear the grim reality and drowned himself in the Milo River on the fifth day of the fifth lunar month, which has become the Dragon Boat Festival in his memory.

Other poems attributed to Qu Yuan include *Nine Hymns* and *Nine Elegies*. The former are songs dedicated to gods or goddesses and written in a form suggestive of drama, in which a male or female shaman donned elaborate costume and make-up, and singing and dancing, invited the god or goddess to an amorous encounter. As sacrifices to the gods were occasions for courtship, the mention of love in these hymns is natural, whether love between man and woman, god and goddess or god and mortal. In *To the God of Cloud* the songstress professes love for the god; in *To the Lord of River Xiang* the god courts the goddess; in *To the Lady of River Xiang*, a lovesick goddess is portrayed in dramatic form. In Chinese poetry love between gods comes after that between man and woman, as opposed to the Greek epic in which the romantic comes before the realistic. There is only one hymn which makes no mention of love, that is the poem praising fallen warriors. In that hymn there is no celebration of heroic deeds and feats of arms usually associated with the epic poetry of the West. In *Ode to the Orange*, one of the *Nine Elegies*, we find the image of an ideal man.

Qu Yuan uses in *Nine Hymns* and *Nine Elegies* a line of four, five or six characters, broken in midline by the insertion of a breathing particle "*xi*" and concluded (usually) with end rhyme. This form is known as Southern Song style.

# III

By the end of the period of the Warring States the king of the Qin State in the northwest had conquered all the other states and founded in 221 B.C. the Qin Dynasty with the king as its first emperor. During his reign scholars were buried alive and classics burned so that no literature was left. About a thousand years later the Tang poet Zhang Jie (837-?) wrote a satirical quatrain called *The Pit Where Emperor Qin Burned the Classics*:

> Smoke of burnt classics gone up with the empire's
>     fall,
> Fortress and rivers could not guard the capital.
> Before the pit turned cold, eastern rebellion
>     spread;
> The leaders of revolt were not scholars well-read.

The leaders of the revolt were General Xiang Yu (see Poem 15) of the State of Chu and Liu Bang (see Poem 16) who defeated Xiang in 202 B.C. and founded the Han Dynasty (206 B.C.-A.D. 220). But it was not the victor but the defeated hero and his beautiful Lady Yu who were glorified in poetry later. For example, Li

Qing-zhao (1084-1151) wrote the following quatrain:

> Be man of men while you're alive;
> Be soul of souls e'en though you're dead.
> Think of Xiang Yu who'd not survive
> His men, whose blood for him was shed.

Lady Yu's name became the title of a song sung from generation to generation. Is it not an irony of history?

During the Han's four hundred years of relative peace and stability, literature and learning flourished after Confucian doctrines had formed the official foundation of the state and the civil service examination system was established under the reign of Emperor Wu or Liu Che (156-87 B.C.). Lyrical works were composed in the Southern Song style that derived from the *Nine Hymns* of *The Verse of Chu*, and used a six- or seven-character line broken in the middle by the breathing particle "*xi*." Emperor Liu Che (see Poem 19) wrote in this form too. But, at variance with the emperor, later poets sang the praise more of his disfavoured general than of His Majesty. For instance, Lu Lun (748-800) described the feats of General Li Guang in his *Border Songs*:

> In gloomy woods grass shivers at wind's howl;
> The general takes it for a tiger's growl.
> He shoots an arrow at a shape in view,
> Only to find at dawn a rock pierced through.

Besides the works assigned to known authors, we have anonymous folk songs which take their name from a government office called the Music Bureau, set up around 120 B.C. by Emperor Wu to collect songs from various parts of the empire. These songs reflect the life and hardships of the common people. Some use lines of irregular length and others use predominately five-character lines, a form which reached its climax during the High Tang period.

# IV

Chinese history has been marked by a recurring cycle of unification, division and reunification. The Han Dynasty founded by Liu Bang in 206 B.C. was overthrown in A.D. 220 and the unified empire split into the Three Kingdoms of Wei in the north, Shu in the west and Wu in the south. The Wei Dynasty was set up by Cao Cao (155-220), who was not only a warlord but also a poet who continued the tradition of *The Book of Poetry* and wrote in the old four-character verse form (see Poem 1). His eldest son Cao Pi succeeded him on the throne, continued the tradition of *The Verse of Chu* and became one of the earliest poets to write in seven-character verse form. Cao Zhi (192-232), younger brother of Cao Pi, was well-known for his literary talent, particularly his five-character verse, which won his father's favour when Cao Zhi was only ten years old and provoked the jealousy of his elder brother, who ordered him, under penalty of death, to write a five-character verse while taking seven paces; it reads:

> Pods burned to cook peas,
> Peas weep in the pot:
> "Grown from the same trees,
> Why boil us so hot?"

A nice example of the poet's wit under pressure, this poem along with the many others composed by Cao Pi, Cao Zhi and their father have established the place of the Three Caos, as they are known in the history of Chinese literature.

In 208 Cao Cao was defeated at Red Cliff by Sun Quan, king of the State of Wu, and Zhou Yu, commander-in-chief of the Wu navy, whom Su Shi (1037-1101) described as follows:

I fancy General Zhou Yu at the height
Of his success, with a plume fan in hand,
In a silk hood, so brave and bright,
Laughing and jesting with his bride fair,
While enemy ships were destroyed as planned
Like castles in the air.

The exploits of Liu Bei, king of Shu, and his prime minister Zhuge Liang were also glorified in later poetry, for example, by Du Fu (712-770) in *The Temple of the Famous Premier of Shu*:

The emperor thrice called on him for nation's
    sake;
The famous premier served heart and soul for
    long years.
Before victory was won he died, which would e'er
    make
All heroes after him wet their sleeves with hot
    tears.

For Chinese intellectuals, Zhou Yu has become the image of an ideal general who can win victory against heavy odds, and Zhuge Liang an ideal minister whose life is entirely devoted to the interest of the nation.

Besides works about king and prince, minister and general, there were also popular ballads such as *A Pair of Peacocks Southeast Fly*, composed around 220. This is a long narrative poem telling how the feudal ethics of the patriarchal clan system destroyed the happiness of a young couple, who were unable to overcome it except in death.

## V

The Three Kingdoms were reunified in 265 by the Jin (265-420), but the decay and collapse of the Han had in some degree discredited the Confucian doctrines and cleared the way for a revival of interest in the transcendental thought of Taoist philosophers. During the Wei and Jin dynasties most scholars tried to escape reality and the best-known poet was Tao Qian (365-427), who retired from official life to a pastoral life of farming and writing and became the archtype of the "hermit poet." Many of his poems described the quiet joys of country life, for instance:

> Among the haunts of men I build my cot,
> There's noise of wheels and hoofs, but I hear not.
> How can it leave upon my mind no trace?
> Secluded heart creates secluded place.
> I pick fence-side chrysanthemums at will
> And leisurely I see the southern hill.

But other poems spoke of famine, drought and similar hardships. The Taoist side of his nature told him he should be content with such a life of seclusion, but his dedication to Confucian ideals kept him longing for the less troubled times of the past when virtue prevailed and a scholar could in good conscience take an active part in state affairs. Unable to attain his ideal, he sought solace in wine and verse, writing in a plain and simple style in a five-character verse form.

In 420 the Jin Dynasty was replaced by the Song, and the empire was split into the Northern and Southern Dynasties (420-589). The Southern emperors worshipped Buddha and built hundreds of Buddhist temples so that Buddhism exercised a predominant influence during the Six Dynasties. This can be seen in the following quatrain:

> Orioles sing amid red blooms and green trees;
> By hills and rills wineshop streamers wave in the
>     breeze.
> Four hundred eighty splendid temples still
>     remain
> Of Southern Dynasties in the mist and the rain.

The poets of that period excelled at describing natural sceneries. For example, Xie Tiao (464-499), whom Li Bai (701-762) admired, wrote the following five-character lines:

> I see from distance high and low
> Winglike tiled roofs in sunset's glow.
> The coloured clouds spread like brocade,
> The river calm as silver braid.

In 589 the Northern and Southern Dynasties were both overthrown by the Sui (589-618), and the well-known *Song of Mulan* appeared, a poem about the first Chinese war heroine, which symbolizes the reunification of the North and the South. But the Sui was a short-lived dynasty, whose second and last emperor was notorious for his life of luxury. The poetry of this period tended to be shallow and mannered, ornate in diction and much given to the use of rhetorical devices such as parallelism, allusion and elegant variation.

## VI

The Tang Dynasty (618-907) was the golden age of Chinese poetry. It may be divided into four periods: Early Tang (618-712), High Tang (713-770), Middle Tang (771-835) and Late Tang (836-907). Early Tang poetry followed the ornate style of the Six Dynasties, but some poets began to break the tradition. For instance, Yu Shi-nan (558-638), whom the emperor highly appreciated, wrote the following five-character quatrain called *The Firefly*:

> You shed a flickering light;
> Your wings are weak in flight.

> Afraid to be unknown,
> At night you gleam alone.

Later, Wang Bo (649-676) and three other poets tried to develop a style of their own and were criticized by their contemporaries. But Du Fu wrote the following seven-character quatrain in support of them:

> Our four great poets have their own creative
>     style;
> You shallow critics may make your remarks
>     unfair,
> But you will perish with your criticism, while
> Their fame will last as the river flows fore'er.

It was Chen Zi-ang (661-702) who succeeded in infusing new vitality into the tradition of the Six Dynasties by returning to the spirit of Han and Wei poetry. He was regarded as a precursor of the High Tang poets.

The High Tang period represented the peak of poetic excellence in the Tang Dynasty. It corresponds roughly to the reign of Emperor Xuan Zong (712-755), a ruler whose early years on the throne were marked by power and splendour and who, as a worshipper of Confucius, wrote the following five-character verse while sacrificing to him:

> For what did you so busily strive, my Sage,
> Expounding hard your doctrine in your age?

Even his favourite Lady Yang could write poems and the following is her seven-character quatrain *Dancing*:

> Silk sleeves are swaying ceaselessly with fragrance
>     spread;
> In autumn mist are floating lotus lilies red.
> Light clouds o'er mountains high ripple with
>     breezes cool;
> Young willow shoots caress water of garden pool.

During the reign of Xuan Zong, all civil service examination candidates were required to compose a regulated verse, so poetry became an indispensable accomplishment and a daily accompaniment to the lives of officials and scholars.

Among the High Tang poets, Wang Chang-ling (698-756) was well-known for his seven-character quatrains, in which we can see the influence of the Six Dynasties palace poetry. The following quatrain on a disfavoured court lady is typical:

> She brings her broom at dawn to dust the golden
> halls
> And strolls about with round fan within the
> palace walls.
> Her rosy colour envies wintry crow's black one,
> Oft bathed in favourable light of royal sun.

Instead of describing the luxurious palace life in flowery poetic style, this quatrain reveals the poet's sympathy with a disfavoured lady whose beauty could not even outshine the ugly crow, so it reads more like *Lament of the Autumn Fan* of the Han Dynasty than a palace poem of the Six Dynasties.

Wang Wei (701-761) was the most important pastoral poet of the High Tang period, best known for his five-character poems. He was a devout Buddhist, a fact that deeply influenced the way in which he viewed the world and his place in it. As a celebrator of the quiet joys of rural life, he followed a line of development earlier explored by Tao Qian, though he wrote with greater calm and detachment than had Tao. For example, his *The Dale of Singing Birds* reads as follows:

> I hear osmanthus blooms fall unenjoyed;
> When night comes, hills dissolve into the void.

The rising moon arouses birds to sing,
Their fitful twitters fill the dale with spring.

He did not assiduously seek out the picturesque
elements in the natural landscape, but rather registered
the scenes about him just as they appeared. No wonder
it is said "in his poetry there is painting and in his
painting there is poetry."

## VII

Li Bai was the best-known poet in Chinese history, a
representative of High Tang culture, the combination
of Northern culture represented by Confucian
philosophy and *The Book of Poetry* and Southern
culture represented by Taoist philosophy and *The
Verse of Chu*. His life may be summed up by the
following quatrain *To Li Bai* written by Du Fu:

When autumn comes, you're drifting still like
    thistledown;
You try to find the way to heaven, but you fail.
In singing mad and drinking dead your days you
    drown.
For whom will fly the roc? For whom will
    leap the whale?

Li Bai could not fulfil his Confucian ideal to serve the
country, spending his later years wandering lonely like
a drifting cloud. Nor could he find spiritual freedom
in Taoism which taught him to seek the way to heaven.
He could but chant poetry and drink wine to drown his
sorrows as described by Du Fu in *Eight Immortal
Drinkers*:

Li Bai could turn sweet nectar into verses fine.
Drunk in the capital, he'd lie in shops of wine.
Even imperial summons proudly he'd decline,

Saying immortals could not leave the drink
    divine.

In Li Bai we have the tragedy of a lonely genius
wandering the earth like an angel fallen from heaven.
When would he realize his aspiration to fly to the
sky like the fabulous roc mentioned by the Taoist
philosopher Zhuang Zi?

Li Bai's poetry is marked by masculine grandeur
(*Watching from Afar the Waterfall on Mount Lu*)
and natural grace (*The Moon over Mount Brow*). His
imagery may be sublime (the giant bird symbolizing
his love of freedom) or graceful (the moon conveying
his sympathy to his banished friend Wang Chang-ling).
His description of natural scenery is characterized by
a swift and fierce imaginative sweep. For instance:

Oh, lightning flashes
And thunder rumbles;
With stunning crashes,
The mountain crumbles.

But he disappoints when describing human feelings
and always compares them to natural phenomena. For
example:

However deep the Lake of Peach Blossom may be,
It's not so deep, O Wang Lun! as your love for me.

He is little given to expressions of despair or bitterness.
His poetry on the whole is calm, at times sunny in
outlook. It appears to grow out of certain convictions
that he held regarding life and art, out of a tireless
search for spiritual freedom and communion with
nature as in Poem 77 (*Sitting Alone Facing Peak
Jingting*), a lively imagination and a deep sensitivity to
beauty (*A Reply to Someone in the Hills*).

Peach blossoms fallen on the running stream pass
  by;
This is an earthly paradise beneath the sky.


# VIII

Du Fu was as great a realistic poet as Li Bai was a
romantic. As Li was called "Poet Immortal," Du was
remembered by posterity as the "Poet Sage" or "Poet
Historian" because he had mirrored in his works the
world he lived in and revealed himself with candour
and passion. While Li cherished now Confucian then
Taoist ideal, Du was imbued with a strong Confucian
sense of duty that compelled him to continue serving
the Tang Dynasty in the hope of assuaging the ills of
the nation. His poetry describes the griefs that famine
and misrule were inflicting upon his countrymen
on the one hand and reproaches those who were
responsible for the misery on the other. For instance,
he wrote on his way from the capital to Fengxian the
following well-known couplet:

The mansions burst with wine and meat;
The poor die frozen in the street.

Li Bai also reproached men in power, but he only said:

How can I stoop and bow before the men in power
And so deny myself a happy hour?

These two examples clearly show Li as subjective
and romantic and Du as objective and realistic.

The same is true of their descriptions of natural
scenery. They both wrote about mountains, but we
find in Li's Mount Skyland an imaginary mountain
"surpassing the Five Peaks" in height, and in Du's
Mount Tai (one of the Five Peaks) "one boundless
green outspread two states." They both described the
Yangtze River, Li as "the endless river rolls beyond the
azure sky," a view only the mind's eye can yield, while

in Du "the endless river rolls its waves from hour to hour," in a description obvious to everyone. They both sailed through the Three Gorges; we find in Li only his own joy, while in Du not only the joy of his family but also that of all the people returning to their homes in the recaptured regions. They both wrote about clouds and birds, but in Li's Peak Jingting we seem to see the poet lonely as the cloud and free as the bird, while in Du's Mount Tai the poet is only an observer of the rising clouds and the fleeting birds. They both described rain, but Li did not like to see it coming "from dark, dark cloud," while Du felt happy to see it "mutely moisten all."

In expressing feelings, Li was more personal and Du more sympathetic. Both of them felt lonely, but Li was detached in his solitude while Du could not free himself from his attachment to the Tang Dynasty, and this is one of the essential differences between them.

Among other High Tang poets, Cen Shen (715-770) was well-known for his frontier verse ("The frozen red flag in the wind won't undulate"). His ballads with descriptions of the harsh climate and rough terrain of the frontier stand in marked contrast to the pastoral poems of Wang Wei.


## IX

If the Early Tang and High Tang periods may be likened to the spring and summer of a year, then the Middle Tang can be compared to autumn, the season of harvest. The revolt of An Lu-shan in 755 had a disastrous effect on the economic and political life of the Tang Dynasty and it never recovered its former stability. In keeping with the changed nature of the times poetry took on an increasingly autumnal air. On the one hand, Wei Ying-wu (737-789) followed the tradition of pastoral poetry (*On the West Stream at Chuzhou*) and on the other, Li Yi (748-827), that of the frontier poems (*On Hearing a Flute at Night Atop the Victor's Wall*). But their poetry had not the tone of exuberance that had marked the earlier decades.

The most important poet of the Middle Tang period was Bai Ju-yi (772-846), who mingled Du Fu's realistic tradition with Li Bai's romanticism (*The Everlasting Regret*), but he also made innovations and wrote "New Music Bureau Ballads" in a style marked by deliberate simplicity (*The White-Haired Palace Maid*). He himself placed high value on his poems of social criticism such as *The Red Cockatoo*:

> Annam has sent us from afar a red cockatoo;
> Coloured like peach-tree blossom, it speaks
>     as men do,
> But it is shut up in a cage with bar on bar
> Just as the learned or eloquent scholars are.

This seven-character quatrain, which reveals the relationship between the ruler and the ruled intellectuals, acts more upon the reason than the emotions and may be considered a forerunner of the didactic poetry of the Song Dynasty. Another seven-character quatrain which reveals the Buddhist influence on the poet reads as follows:

> Studying the Buddhist doctrine of emptiness, I
>     find
> The way to still all common states of mind ...

But the great Buddhist influence revolted another Confucian innovator Han Yu (768-824), who submitted to the emperor a memorial in which he reprimanded His Majesty for his devotion to Buddhism and was exiled eight thousand miles away (*Written for My Grandnephew at the Blue Pass*).

Bai Ju-yi was the most prolific of the Middle Tang poets. As Liu Yu-xi (772-842), he composed "Bamboo-Branch Songs" and "Willow-Branch Songs,"

which are early forms of tuned poetry, that is, a poem
or lyric written to a certain tune whose title refers
simply to the metrical pattern and in most cases has
nothing to do with the poem's content. The tuned lyric
marked by lines of varying length came to prominence
in the Middle Tang period. For example, Zhang
Zhi-he's (730-810) *A Fisherman's Song* was so
widespread that even the Japanese emperor (r.
804-832) wrote five lyrics to the same tune. Zhang's
lyric is pastoral, Liu's *Ripples Sifting Sand* realistic
and Bai's *A Flower in the Haze* symbolic.

## X

Li He (790-816) who followed the romantic tradition
of Qu Yuan and Li Bai, and whose rich, allusion-laden
poetry is obscure and even depressing, may be regarded
as precursor of Late Tang poets. If the major poets of
the High Tang were Li Bai and Du Fu, then those of
the Late Tang were another Li and Du, that is, Du Mu
(803-852) and Li Shang-yin (812-858).

    Du Mu has shunned in his poetry "the ornate and
the strange" on the one hand and "the commonplace
and the vulgar" on the other. His seven-character
quatrains are admired for their visual immediacy and
delicacy of feeling. For instance, one of his farewell
poems reads:

> Deep, deep our love, too deep to show.
> Deep, deep we drink; silent we grow.
> The candle grieves to see us part;
> It melts in tears with burnt-out heart.

    Li Shang-yin was perhaps the most influential of
all the Late Tang poets. His seven-character regulated
verse reads like Du Fu's and Han Yu's in syntax and
structure, and like Li He's in diction and allusiveness.
He is well-known for his ambiguous or obscure poems,

often untitled, dealing with clandestine love. He was the first poet to write love poems in the modern sense and has left to posterity such unforgettable couplets as:

> The silkworm till its death spins silk from
>   lovesick heart;
> The candle when consumed has no more tears to
>   shed.
> The setting sun appears sublime,
> But O! 'Tis near its dying time.

The second couplet may be said to be the epitome of Late Tang poetry.

Wen Ting-yun (813-870) was the most important lyricist or composer of tuned lyrics of the Late Tang; he transformed them from mere songs of entertainment to verse of high literary quality. In his lyrics two main styles predominate: a richly embellished depiction of the abandoned woman as opposed to the court lady in the palace poem, and a simple narration in the folk song manner as represented by *Dreaming of the South*.

Wei Zhuang (836-910) was another important lyricist of the period of transition. His tuned lyrics are straightforward, narrative and colloquial, directly expressing personal feelings and autobiographical details as opposed to Wen's indirect depiction of feminine feelings. What he adds to the tuned lyric reveals a reaction against the ornate style of Wen, who excels in writing poems with implicit meaning, while Wei is famed for explicit poetry.

In 881, Huang Chao (?-884) led an army of sixty thousand peasant rebels into the Tang capital and proclaimed himself emperor. He expressed his ambition in *The Chrysanthemum*, with whose "golden armour plates" came the end of the Tang Dynasty.

## XI

After the downfall of the Tang in 907, five short-lived
dynasties were successively founded and overthrown
from 907 to 960, and the unified empire was
dismembered into ten independent sovereign states, of
which the State of Shu in the west and that of the
Southern Tang in the east were well-known for their
literary achievements. When the regulated Tang verse
could no longer adequately express man's more refined
and delicate feelings, the tuned lyric of irregular
line-length took its place and evolved into a major
literary genre during the Five Dynasties. The literary
aspect of the tuned lyric was derived from the
five-character and seven-character lines of the
regulated verse, the musical aspect from the popular
songs and the tunes introduced from Central Asia,
India and Myanmar. For example, *The Buddhist
Dancers*, one of the most popular tunes, was said to be
a song in praise of the hairdress of the Myanmar
empress of the time. So the tuned lyric may be
considered as a result of intercultural communication.

As mentioned above, the states of Shu and
Southern Tang were two cultural centres during the
Five Dynasties period. In the former the first
anthology of tuned lyrics appeared in 940, most of
which can be called boudoir poetry in that it described
beautiful heart-broken women in elegant chambers
keeping cold, lonely beds beside a dimming candle or
a solitary screen, in the waning spring or the dead of
night, their lovers having gone far, far away.

Li Yu (937-978), the last ruler of the Southern
Tang (937-975), represents the highest achievement of
the lyric poets during the Five Dynasties period. His
unusual accomplishment was closely related to his
personal experiences. In his early years, as monarch, he
indulged in a luxurious life at court; after losing his
kingdom to the Song emperor in 976 and becoming a
political prisoner in the Song capital, he lived a life of

suffering until his death. His tragedy may be summed up in his tuned lyric written to the tune of *Dance of the Cavalry*, in which the expanse of his lost kingdom symbolizes the limitless extent of the universe and the short history of his dynasty becomes a universal symbol of the time past. The dominant theme in his lyric is no longer confined to the experiences of the inner chamber, but extends to embrace the historical dimension of a kingdom and the vast expanse of an empire. His individual experiences seem to gain a universal importance. When compared with Wen and Wei, Li's poetry is more universal. Wen's lyrics are descriptive and static, Wei's narrative and active, while Li's more personal and emotional verses seem to view his own suffering in light of the destiny of all mankind. If Wen's lyrics are written with coloured ink and Wei's with bitter tears, then Li's are composed of his heart's blood.

## XII

The tuned lyrics predominant in the Five Dynasties were short tunes divided into two stanzas and containing no more than 62 characters. The lyricists of the Northern Song (960-1127) included high officials and even prime ministers, who brought poetry into closer contact with the life of prosperous society in all its aspects—secular, intellectual and artistic. Premier Yan Shu (991-1055) and his son Yan Ji-dao (1030-1106) were both good at composing short tunes. Professor Chia-ying Yeh, who calls the son "poet of feeling" and the father "poet of intellect," says in *Song Without Music*: "The one responds passively to life, registering experience as pure feeling; the other does not simply experience reality, he contributes a ray of understanding to his experience. The response of the former suffers from its narrowness, where the latter has the advantage of breadth. Where the response is purely emotional, the poetry conveys emotion but lacks thought, making for superficiality, while the one who can illuminate his subject will include thought with his feelings, and the result is greater depth. Consider these lines by Yan Shu: Deeply I sigh for faded flowers' fall in vain/Vaguely I seem to know the swallows come again." The observation of seasonal change is not just the occasion for an emotional response. The poet perceives a pattern, a contrast or a repetition, that gives a rational basis for the emotion.

Yan Shu may be regarded as the leader of early Northern Song poets, among whom figured Fan Zhong-yan (989-1052), well-known for the quote that an ideal minister should be "first in worrying about the troubles of the world and last in enjoying its pleasures," and also known for his frontier lyrics. Ouyang Xiu (1007-1072), who sought spiritual sublimation in prose and emotional satisfaction in verse, was successful in enlarging the themes and the language of love poetry.

The short lyrics these poets wrote were as restricted in form as in content, for the restriction in form had its impact on content. It was Liu Yong (987-1053) who began to compose long lyrics or slow tunes, whose length ranges from 70 to 240 characters and which afford sufficient room for undulation and amplification. With the skilful use of this diversified form, he was able to transcend such conventional motifs as sorrows of love or remorse over separation and diverge from the domestic and the personal by giving voice to a deeper and more complex layer of meaning, to a wider horizon of the spiritual world, such as the sense of desolation and loftiness evoked by watching distant places in *Eight Beats of Ganzhou Song*. Thus in his hand the spirit and the outlook of the tuned lyric underwent a radical change, the rise of the long tunes becoming a major event in the evolution of the lyric.

## XIII

The most important poet and lyricist of the Song Dynasty was Su Shi (Su Dong-po, 1037-1101). If the development of the tuned lyric in form may be attributed to Liu Yong, then its growth in content must be credited to Su Shi, who created the lyric in the mode of Tang poetry and in so doing broadened its scope and elevated its status to the extent that "there is no idea which cannot be expressed and there is no subject which cannot be treated" in his lyrics. His style is exuberant and spontaneous, characterized by his virile, unrestrained nature. His poetic diction ranges from colloquialism to classical expressions. His philosophy represents a combination of Confucianism and Taoism: "to serve the crown and to attain great renown" (*Spring in the Garden of Qin*) is his Confucian ideal and "to retire as times require" (*ibid.*), and to be detached from gain and loss, his Taoist ideal. His philosophy can be seen in the following long lyric written to the tune of *Congratulations to the Bridegroom*:

> Young swallows fly along the painted eave
> Which none perceive.
> The shade of plane-trees keeps away
> The hot noonday
> And brings an evening fresh and cool
> For the bathing lady beautiful.
> She flirts a round fan of silk made,
> Both fan and hand as white as jade.
> Tired by and by,
> She falls asleep with lonely sigh.
> Who's knocking at the curtained door
> That she can dream sweet dreams no more?
> It is the gentle breeze who
> Is again swaying green bamboo.

The pomegranate opens half her lips
Which look like wrinkled crimson strips;
When all the fickle flowers fade,
Alone she'll be the Beauty's maid.
How charming in her blooming branch, behold!
A fragrant heart seems wrapped a thousandfold.
But she's afraid to be surprised by western breeze
Which withers all the green leaves on the trees.
When you come to drink to the flower fair,
To see her withered too you cannot bear.
Then tears and flowers
Would fall in showers.

The bathing Beauty is no longer the abandoned lady of palace poems, but an image of the purified soul of the disfavoured poet still dreaming of his ideal unfulfilled, the pomegranate a symbol of the purified lady envied by all the fickle flowers. Here we see three images combined into one, that of a disappointed but not disillusioned intellectual.

Su Shi was considered to be the leader of the "heroic" school of lyrics, but he was also an innovator in writing lyrics of "delicate restraint," and Qin Guan (1049-1100), one of his followers, was regarded as representative of the "delicate" school. He was well-known for the following couplet:

If love between both sides can last for aye,
Why need they stay together night and day?

On the other hand, Zhou Bang-yan (1056-1121), one of Liu Yong's followers, inherited the form from the master while at the same time surpassing his achievements. "While Su Shi remained an observer in creating a metaphorical relation between external objects and universal human feelings, Zhou developed a situation of poetic empathy in which the lyric self maintains a symbolic correspondence with external objects" (Kang-i Sun's *Evolution of Chinese Tz'u*

*Poetry*). It is interesting to note that Zhou was once the rival of Emperor Hui Zong (Zhao Ji, 1082-1135) for the love of a singing girl Li Shi-shi (*Wandering of a Youth*). The emperor was himself a lyricist and wrote *Apricot Seen in the North* to the tune of *Hillside Pavilion* (see Poem 272) when he was a captive sent to the north by the Jurchen invaders. The descendant of the Song emperor who had captured Li Yu and put him to death was in turn captured and put to death by the Jurchen aggressors. Is it not true to say that justice has a long arm?

## XIV

In 1125 when the Jurchen invaders marched south, the Song was forced to move its capital from Kaifeng to Hangzhou, south of the Yangtze River; that marked the beginning of the Southern Song Dynasty (1127-1279). Many patriots spoke out against the humiliation and called for military action to remedy it, thus Southern Song poetry possessed a patriotic fervour, of which General Yue Fei's (1103-1141) *The River All Red* is typical.

Li Qing-zhao (1084-1151), who lived in the intervening period between the Northern and Southern Song, was the most remarkable lyric poetess of the Song Dynasty. Her lyrics recollect nostalgically her happy life in Kaifeng and reveal her distress in Hangzhou. "Her attempt to establish life in poetry was for her a stay against time, a surety to blot out oblivion. She tried to recapture the past, to preserve the present...." (*Sunflower Splendour*).

Lu You (1125-1210) was the best-known patriotic poet of the Southern Song. Even on his deathbed, he wrote the following quatrain exhorting his sons not to fail to report to his spirit at family sacrifices the news of the eventual recovery of the lost territory:

After my death I know for me all hopes are vain,
But still I'm grieved to see our country not unite.
When royal armies recover the Central Plain,
Do not forget to tell your sire in sacred rite!

Xin Qi-ji (1140-1207) was regarded as the most important lyric poet of the Southern Song Dynasty. He was a successor to Su Shi, continuing his thematic emphasis while at the same time putting a tighter rein on prosody than his master. It was not until his appearance that the tuned lyric flourished and reached its apex. His reputation as the best lyric poet of the "powerful and free" school rests on his heroic sentiments expressed in such lyrics as *The Partridge Sky* and *Dance of the Cavalry*.

On the other hand, among the lyric poets of the school of "delicate restraint," the best-known were Jiang Kui (1155-1221) and Wu Wen-ying (1200-1260). Successors to Zhou Bang-yan, they had certain common features, such as their painstaking choice of words and phrases, and the great attention they paid to the music and the description of subtle feeling. But the content of their poems tended to be ambiguous and empty, full of ornate classical allusions. As the tuned lyric became more and more concerned with technical details of embellishment, it gradually lost its vitality.

Towards the end of the Southern Song, the best-known poet of the "heroic" school was Wen Tian-xiang (1236-1282), prime minister who led the royalist army to fight the Tartar invaders in 1275. Defeated and captured, he wrote the following verse on his way to Yanjing (present-day Beijing):

But I'll come back with blood oozing in cuckoo's
cry.

He was executed in 1282 and with his death came the end of the Southern Song Dynasty.

## XV

During the one century of Mongol rule in the Yuan period (1279-1368), new musical melodies and new poetic genres emerged: song-poems, or non-dramatic songs, and dramatic songs. The new forms admit freely the use of everyday colloquial speech, the idiom and slang of the common people and extra words in addition to what was required by the melody. Writers of non-dramatic songs were skilled in their descriptions of sceneries and situations, persons and objects (though sometimes trivial and humorous) and thoughts and sentiments. But as a whole, the song-poem is basically lyrical in nature. On the other hand, dramatic songs are not only lyrical but also narrative. The most important writer of dramatic songs was Wang Shi-fu whose *Romance of the Western Chamber* contains a narrative part in prose and a lyrical part in verse. So the Yuan period may be considered one of transition from the predominance of poetry to that of prose. During the Ming Dynasty (1368-1644) narrative prose predominated over lyrical poetry, and it was not until the appearance of *A Dream of Red Mansions* in the Qing period (1644-1911) that the lyrical became as important as, if not more important than the narrative, but that question goes beyond the scope of the present book.

# ZHOU DYNASTY
## (1112-256 B.C.)

## *"THE BOOK OF POETRY"*
### *(Compiled 770-476 B.C.)*

### A Fair Maiden

By riverside are cooing
A pair of turtledoves;
A good young man is wooing
A maiden fair he loves.

Water flows left and right
Of cresses here and there;
The youth yearns day and night
For the good maiden fair.

His yearning grows so strong
He cannot fall asleep;
He tosses all night long,
So deep in love, so deep!

Now gather left and right
The cresses sweet and tender;
O lute, play music bright
For the bride fair and slender!

Feast friends at left and right
On cresses cooked so tender;
O bells and drums, delight
The bride so fair and slender!

## The Fruits from Mume Tree Fall

The fruits from mume tree fall,
One-third of them away.
If you love me at all,
Woo me a lucky day!

The fruits from mume tree fall,
Two-thirds of them away.
If you love me at all,
Woo me this very day!

The fruits from mume tree fall,
Now all of them away.
If you love me at all,
You need not woo but say!


## My Quiet Maiden

My quiet maiden is fair and tall;
She waits for me at the corner wall.
Evasive, she can be found nowhere;
Scratching my head, I seek here and there.

Beautiful is my quiet lass;
She gives me a blade of crimson grass.
The crimson grass spreads a rosy light;
I love the grass so fair and bright.

My maiden comes back from the mead;
She gives me a beautiful rare reed.
It's beautiful not because it's rare;
But it's the gift of my maiden fair.

## The Faithless Man

A man seemed free from guile,
In trade he wore a smile.
He'd barter cloth for thread;
No, to me he'd be wed.
We went across the ford;
I'd not give him my word.
I said by hillside green,
"You have no go-between.
Try to find one, I pray.
In autumn be the day!"

I climbed the wall to wait
To see him pass the gate.
I did not see him pass;
My tears streamed down, alas!
I saw him passing by,
I'd laugh with joy and cry.
Both reed and tortoise shell
Foretold all would be well.
"Come with your cart," I said.
"To you I will be wed."

How fresh were mulberries
With their fruits on the trees!
Beware, O turtledove,
Eat not the fruits you love,
For they'll intoxicate.
Do not repent too late!
Man may do what he will,
He can atone it still.
The wrong a woman's done
No man will e'er condone.

The mulberries appear
With yellow leaves and sear.
E'er since he married me,
I've shared his poverty.

Desert'd, from him I part,
The flood has wet my cart.
I have done nothing wrong;
He changes all along.
He's fickle to excess,
Capricious, pitiless.

Three years I was his wife
And led a toilsome life.
Each day I early rose,
And late I sought repose.
He thought it not enough
And began to become rough.
My brothers did not know,
Their jeers at me would go.
Mutely I ruminate
And then deplore my fate.

I'd live with him in vain;
I had cause to complain.
I love the ford of yore
And the wide rivershore.
When we were girl and boy,
We'd talk and laugh with joy.
He pledged to me his troth.
Could he forget his oath?
He's forgot what he swore.
Should I say any more?

## My Man's Away

My man's away to serve the state;
I can't anticipate
How long he will there stay
Nor when he'll be on homeward way.
The sun is setting in the west,
The fowls are roosting in their nest,
The sheep and cattle come to rest.

To serve the state my man's away.
How can I not miss him night and day?

My man's away to serve the state;
I can't anticipate
When we'll again have met.
The sun's already set,
The fowls are roosting in their nest,
The sheep and cattle come to rest.
To serve the state my man's away.
Keep him from hunger and thirst, I pray!

## Cock's Crow, Hark!

The wife says, "Cock's crow, hark!"
The man says, "It's still dark."
"Rise and look at the night;
The morning star shines bright."
"Wild geese and duck will fly;
I'll shoot them down from high."

"At shooting you are good;
I'll dress the game as food.
Together we'll drink wine,
And live to ninety-nine.
With zither by our side,
At peace we shall abide."

"I know your wifely care,
I'll give you pearls to wear.
I know your will to obey.
Can pearls and jade repay?
I know your steadfast love,
I value nothing above."

## The Cock Is Crowing

"Wake up, the cock is crowing,
The lords to court are going."
"It's not the cock that cries,
But humming of the flies."

"The east is brightening,
The court is in full swing."
"It's not the east that's bright,
But the moon shedding light."

"The humming insects fly,
It's sweet in bed to lie.
But lords will leave the hall.
Do not displease them all!"

## Comradeship

Are you not battle-drest?
Let's share the plate for breast.
We shall go up the line.
Let's make our spears and lances shine.
Your foe is mine.

Are you not battle-drest?
Let's share the coat and vest.
We shall go up the line.
Let's make our halberds shine.
Your work is mine.

Are you not battle-drest?
Let's share the kilt, the rest.
We shall go up the line.
Let's make our armour shine.
We'll march in line.

## Homecoming After the War

When I left here,
Willows shed tear.
Now I come back
On snowy track.
Long, long the way;
Hard, hard the day.
My grief o'erflows.
Who knows? Who knows!

## Hunting

Well built and firm our car,
Well match'd our horses are.
We yoke four horses strong
And eastward drive along.

Splendid our hunting car;
Sturdy our horses are.
Eastward the grasslands spread;
We drive and hunt ahead.

Our master sallies out,
The picked footmen shout.
With banners they display,
They start to chase the prey.

They drive the four-horsed car.
How strong the horses are!
They're dressed in bright array
As on an audience day.

Thimbles and armlets fit;
Arrows from bows will hit.
Together archers shoot;
In piles lie birds and brute.

They drive four horses bay,
No side steeds swerve or sway.
The car straightforward goes;
The arrows fall like blows.

The homing horses neigh,
The footmen flags display.
The archers are so skilled,
With game the kitchen's filled.

Our lord's on homeward way;
He's fairly won the day.
Not words but deeds are good;
In him there's true manhood.

## QU YUAN (340-278 B.C.)

### To the God of Cloud

Bathed in orchid-scented dews
And dressed in robes of varied hues,
With fleecy hair you slowly rise
To beautify the morning skies.

Within your deathless hall at noon
Your whiteness rivals sun and moon.
The dragon is your charioteer;
You waft and wander far and near.

In silver drops you come with rain;
On wings of wind you rise again.
You gaze upon the land with ease;
You float o'er and beyond Four Seas.

Longing for you, I can't but sigh,
My yearning heart to you would fly.

## To the Lord of River Xiang

Why don't you come, still hesitating?
For whom on midway isle are you waiting?
Fair and duly adorned, I float
On rapid stream my cassia boat.
I bid the waves more slowly go
And the river tranquilly flow.
I wait for you who have not come;
Playing my flute, with grief I'm numb.

In dragon boat for north I make
And zigzag to Dongting Lake.
Ivy behind, lotus before,
Orchid for flag, cedar for oar,
I gaze on the lake's farthest side;
My soul can't cross the river wide.
Across the river I can't fly;
For my distress my handmaids sigh.
My tears stream down and slowly flow;
Longing for you, I hide my woe.

With orchid rudder and cassia oar,
I break the ice and snow before,
As plucking ivy from the stream
Or lotus from trees in a dream.
The go-between cannot unite
Two divided hearts whose love is light,
As on a shallow stream can't float
Even a winged dragon boat.
Faithless, you are deceiving me;
Breaking our tryst, you say you're not free.

At dawn I drive my cab by riverside;
At eve on northern isle I stop my ride.
Under the eaves the birds repose;
Around the house the river flows.
I throw in water my jade rings
And cast away my offerings.

I pluck sweet flowers on the isle
And give them to maids poor but not vile.
Lost time cannot be found again;
From thinking of you I'd refrain.


## To the Lady of River Xiang

On Northern Isle descends my dear,
But I am grieved to see not clear.
The ceaseless autumn breeze grieves
The Dongting waves with fallen leaves.
I gaze afar 'mid clover white
And wait for our tryst at twilight.
Among the reeds can birds be free?
What can a net do on the tree?
White clover grows beside the creek;
I long for you but dare not speak.
I gaze afar, my beloved one,
I see but rippling water run.
Could deer find food within the door?
What could a dragon do ashore?
At dawn by riverside I urge my steed;
At dusk across the western stream I speed.
For you bid me to come today;
Together we're to ride away.

A midstream palace shall be made,
O'er its roof lotus weave a shade.
In purple court thyme decks the wall,
With fragrant pepper spread the hall.
Pillars of cassia stand upright,
And rooms smell sweet with clover white.
We weave the ivy into a screen
And spread the ground with its leaves green.
The cornerstones shall be white jade,
And fragrance of orchids shall not fade.
On lotus roof let vetch be found
And fresh azaleas around.

The courtyard filled with herbs so fair,
The corridor with perfume rare.
All gods will come from mountains high
Like clouds that overspread the sky.

I throw, when waking from my dream,
My shirt with sleeves into the stream.
I pluck sweet flowers on the bay,
I'd give to strangers far away.
Lost time can't oft be found again,
From thinking of you I'd refrain.

## For Those Fallen for the Country

We take our southern spears and don our coats of mail;
When chariot axles clash, with daggers we assail.
Banners obscure the sun, the foe roll up like cloud,
Arrows fall thick; forward press our warriors proud.
Our line is broken through, our position o'errun,
My left-hand horse is killed and wounded my
     right-hand one.
The fallen horses block my wheels and I am stayed;
In vain I beat the sounding drum with rods of jade.
By angry powers' order our men should be slain,
And here and there our warriors' corpses strew the
     plain.
They came out not to return to where they belong;
The battlefield's so vast, their homeward way so long.
With sword in hand and long bow captured from the
     west,
Though head and body sever, their heart's not
     repressed.
They were indeed courageous and ready to fight,
And steadfast to the end, undaunted by armed might.
Their spirit deathless is, although their blood was shed,
Captains among the ghosts, heroes among the dead!

# HAN DYNASTY
## (206 B.C.-A.D. 220)

## *XIANG YU (232-202 B.C.)* *

**The Last Song**

I could pull down a mountain with my might,
My fortune wanes and e'en my steed won't fight.
Whether my steed will fight, I do not care.
What can I do with you, my lady fair?

## *LIU BANG (256-195 B.C.)* **

**Song of the Big Wind**

A big wind rises, clouds are driven away.
Home am I now the world is under my sway.
Where are brave men to guard the four frontiers today!

**"Nineteen Old Poems"**

**(I)**

You travel on and on
And leave me all alone.
Away ten thousand li,

---

* Xiang Yu the conqueror fought against Liu Bang for the throne.
Defeated, he and his favourite Lady Yu committed suicide. The lady
was so beautiful that her name became a tune title: "The Beautiful
Lady Yu."
** First emperor of the Han Dynasty (206 B.C.-A.D. 220).

At the end of the sea.
Severed by hard, long way,
Oh, can we meet someday?
Northern steeds love cold breeze,
And southern birds warm trees.
The farther you are away,
The thinner I am each day.
The cloud has veiled the sun;
You won't come back, dear one.
Missing you makes me old;
Soon comes the winter cold.
Alas! Of me you're quit.
I hope you will keep fit.

## "FOLK SONGS"

### The Roadside Mulberry

The rising sun from southeast nook
Shines on the house of Qin, who
Has a daughter of lovely looks;
She calls herself Luofu.
She picks mulberry leaves still new
To feed silkworms in southern nook,
Her basket's bound with silk thread blue,
Of laurel bough is made a hook.
Her hair is dressed in pretty braid,
Like moonbeams her pearl earrings shine,
Of yellow silk her apron's made,
Her cloak of purple damask fine.

When she is seen by passers-by,
They stroke their beards and there take root;
When she appears in young men's eye,
They doff their caps and make salute.
The ploughman thinks not of his plough,
The hoer leaves in field his hoe.

Back, they find fault with their wives now,
For they have seen Luofu aglow.

From the south comes the governor,
Whose carriage and five stop and stay.
He sends men to inquire of her.
"Who are you, pretty maid?" ask they.

"I call my humble self Luofu."
"Pretty Luofu, how old are you?"
"My age is still less than a score,
But much more than fifteen, much more."
"Our lord bids us to ask Luofu,
Will you ride with our lord, will you?"

Luofu steps forth and makes reply:
"What nonsense you are talking. Why,
Your Excellency has his wife;
I have my husband dear for life.
There are more than a thousand steeds
In the east that my husband leads."

"But how can I your husband know?"
"Ah, by his horse as white as snow,
Whose tail is tied with a blue thread,
With golden halters round its head;
By the sword with its hilt of jade,
For which its weight in gold he paid.

"At fifteen he was a junior clerk;
At twenty he did a courtier's work;
At thirty he wore chamberlain's gown;
At forty he was lord of a town.

"His face and skin are white and fair,
A rather long beard he does wear.
In the court he walks to and fro,
And goes to the palace with steps slow.

Among the thousands in the hall,
He's deemed the most distinguished of all."


## LIU CHE (156-87 B.C.) *

### Song of the Autumn Wind

The autumn wind rises and white clouds fly,
When leaves turn yellow, wild geese head for southern
  sky.
The orchids and chrysanthemums still sweeten the air.
Oh, how can I forget my lady sweet and fair!
I go aboard a bark to cross the river long;
It reaches midstream when I see the waves rise white.
The flutes and drums keep time to the rowers' song,
But sorrow comes when pleasure reaches its height.
How long will youth endure when old age is in sight!


## LADY BAN **

### Lament of the Autumn Fan

Fresh from the weaver's loom, O silk so white,
As clear as frost, as winter snow as bright.
Fashioned into a fan, token of love,
You are as round as brilliant moon above.
In my lord's sleeve when in or out he goes,
You wave and shake and a light wind blows.
I fear when comes the autumn day,
And chilling wind drives summer heat away,
You'll be discarded to a lonely place,
And with my lord fall into disgrace.

---

* Emperor Wu of the Han Dynasty, who wrote the elegy for his
favourite Lady Li.
** The favourite of Emperor Cheng of the Han Dynasty, who fell
into disgrace like the autumn fan, which has become a symbol of
disgrace since then.

# THREE KINGDOMS
(220-280)


## *CAO CAO (155-220)* *

### The Sea

I come to view the boundless ocean
From Stony Hill on eastern shore.
Its water rolls in rhythmic motion,
And islands stand amid its roar.

Tree on tree grows from peak to peak;
Grass on grass looks lush far and nigh.
The autumn wind blows drear and bleak;
The monstrous billows surge up high.

The sun by day, the moon by night
Appear to rise up from the deep.
The Milky Way with stars so bright
Sinks down into the sea in sleep.

How happy I feel at this sight!
I croon this poem in delight.


## *CAO PI (186-226)*

### On the Death of My Father**

Raising my eyes, I see his screen;
Bending my head, his table clean.

---

* Sovereign of the Kingdom of Wei.
** Cao Cao (155-220), King of Wei.

16

These things are there just as before,
The man who owned them is no more.
Suddenly his spirit has flown
And left me fatherless, alone.
Who'd look to me? On whom rely?
Tear upon tear streams from my eye.
The deer are bleating here and there,
They feed the young ones in their care.
The birds are flying east and west,
Feeding the nestlings in the nest.
Alone I'm desolate and drear,
Severed from the father I revere.
Deep in my heart grief overflows,
But no one knows, no one knows.
'Tis said that sorrow makes us old
And early grow white hair. Behold!
For the deceased I wail and sigh;
If the good live long, why should he die!

## CAO ZHI (192-232)*

### Written While Taking Seven Paces

Pods burned to cook peas,
Peas weep in the pot:
"Grown from the same trees,
Why boil us so hot?"

---

* Cao Zhi was the younger brother of Cao Pi who, after coming to the throne, ordered him to compose a poem while taking seven paces and he wrote this quatrain in which pods and peas allude to brothers at odds.

## *ANONYMOUS*

### A Pair of Peacocks Southeast Fly

*During the reign of Jian'an (196-219) in the Eastern Han Dynasty there was a local official in the prefecture of Lujiang called Jiao Zhong-qing, whose wife, Liu Lan-zhi, was sent away by his mother and vowed never to marry again. Compelled by her family to break her vow, she had no recourse but to drown herself in a pool. On hearing the news, Zhong-qing hanged himself on a tree in the courtyard. The following poem was composed by contemporaries in their memory.*

A pair of peacocks southeast fly;
At each mile they look back and cry.

"I could weave," said Lan-zhi, "at thirteen
And learned to cut clothes at fourteen;
At fifteen to play music light;
At sixteen to read and to write.
At seventeen to you I was wed.
What an austere life I have led!

"You're an official far away;
I toil as housewife night and day.
At daybreak I begin to weave;
At night the loom I dare not leave.
I've finished five rolls in three days,
Yet I am blamed for my delays.
Not that my work is done too slow,
But hard your housewife's role does grow.
If Mother thinks I am no good,
What use to stay, although I would?
Will you come and to Mother say,
Send me back home without delay?"

Jiao Zhong-qing came home at her call
And said to his mother in the hall,
"I'm destined for a humble life;
By fortune I have this good wife.
We've shared the pillow, mat and bed,
And we'll be man and wife till dead.
We've lived together but three years,
Which not too long to me appears.
She has done nothing wrong, I find.
Why should you be to her unkind?"

His mother said then in reply,
"You are indeed shortsighted. Why,
This wife of yours with me goes ill;
She always does whate'er she will.
I've been offended by her for long.
How dare you say she's done no wrong?
In the east there's a match for you,
A maiden whose name's Qin Luo-fu,
A peerless beauty of this land.
I'll go for you to ask her hand.
Now send your slut out of our door!
She should not stay here any more."

Zhong-qing knelt down with trunk erect
And said to her with due respect,
"If you should send away my wife,
I won't remarry all my life."
The mother was angry at his word;
Her strumming on the stool was heard.
"Has filial reverence come to nil?
Defend your wife against my will!
You are such an ungrateful son!
Of your request I will grant none."

Zhong-qing dared not speak any more,
But bowed and entered his own door.
He tells his wife when she appears,
His voice choked so with bitter tears,

"Not that I would send you away,
But Mother won't allow you to stay.
Return to your brother's house, so
That to my office I may go.
When I have finished my work, then
I'll come and fetch you home again.
Do not be grieved to say adieu,
But keep in mind what I've told you!"

"Nay, make no care to come for me!"
To her husband addresses she.
"One early spring day, I recall,
I left home for your entrance hall.
I've done what Mother ordered me.
Dare I be careless and carefree?
I do hard labour day and night;
Alone I toil with all my might.
I think I have done nothing wrong,
Still with Mother I can't get along.
To what avail to talk about
Returning now I'm driven out!

"I'll leave my jacket of brocade,
Whose lacings bright of gold are made,
And my canopy of gauze red,
Whose four corners with perfume spread,
And sixty trunks and coffers tied
With silken threads all in green dyed,
Where different things you will find;
Not two of them are of a kind.
They are as cheap as I, it's true,
Not good enough for your spouse new.
So as gifts you may share them out,
As we can't meet again, no doubt.
Keep them in memory of me!
Forgetful we can never be."

At dawn she rose at the cockcrow
And made up with care, ready to go.

She put on an embroidered gown
And checked it over, up and down.
She put on shoes made of brocade,
Of tortoise shell her hairpin's made.
Her waist was girt with girdle white,
Her earrings shone like moonlight bright.
She had tapering finger tips,
Like rubies were her rouged lips.
She moved at slow and easy pace,
Unrivalled in the human race.

She came to his mother in the hall,
Who said no tender words at all.
"While young, before I was a spouse,
I lived but in a country house.
Not well instructed or wide read,
For noble heir I was ill-bred.
Though kindly you have treated me,
Yet I'm not dutiful," said she,
"So I must go back in despair,
Leaving to you all household care."

She said to his sister good-bye;
Bitter tears trickled from her eye.
"When your brother and I were wed,
You came around our nuptial bed.
You are as tall as I today,
When I am to be driven away.
Take good care of your mother old,
And take good care of your household!
When maidens hold their festive day,
Do not forget me while you play."
She went out and got on the cart;
Tears streamed down, heavy was her heart.

Jiao Zhong-qing rides before, his mind
Turning to his wife's cart behind.
The cart's rumble's heard to repeat,
The husband stops where four roads meet.

He gets down from his horse, comes near
His wife and whispers in her ear,
"I swear not to leave you long, my spouse.
Return now to your brother's house.
When I have finished my work, then
I'll come and fetch you home again.
I swear to heaven high above
That forever will last our love."

Lan-zhi says to her husband dear,
"I'm touched by your love sincere.
If I'm engraved deep in your mind,
Come then in time and not behind!
If as the rock your love is strong,
Then mine as creeping vine is long.
The vine's resistant as silk thread;
No one could lift a rock o'erhead.
But my brother's temper is hot,
Look on me kindly he will not.
I am afraid he'll never care
What I like, and it's hard to bear."
They wave their hands with broken heart,
From each other they will not part.

Lan-zhi came to her mother's place,
Feeling embarrassed in disgrace.
Her mother clapped loud in surprise:
"How can you come back in this guise!
You were taught to weave at thirteen;
To cut the clothes at fourteen;
At fifteen to play music light;
At sixteen to perform the rite.
At seventeen you were a bride;
By your husband you should abide.
Had you done nothing wrong at all,
Why come back alone to my hall?"
Lan-zhi told her mother the truth,
Who was moved to tears, full of ruth.

She had been back many a day,
A go-between then came to say,
"Our magistrate has a third son,
Whose good looks are second to none.
Though at eighteen or nineteen years,
For eloquence he has no peers."
Her mother said to her, "Consent
To this proposal benevolent!"
But she only answered in tears,
"Can I forget my married years?
My husband vowed when we parted then,
Never should we sever again.
If I should break my word today,
I would regret for e'er and aye.
Will you please tell the go-between
Gently and clearly what I mean?"
Her mother told the messenger,
"This humble daughter of mine, sir,
Sent back by an official of late,
Can't match a son of magistrate.
Why not inquire another house
Where may be found a better spouse?"

No sooner had gone this messenger
Than came one from the governor.
"You have a daughter fair," said he,
"Of an official's family.
Our governor has a fifth son,
Unmarried, he's a handsome one.
My lord's secretary asked me
His lordship's go-between to be.
I was told to say openly
I come for my lord's family.
His son will have your daughter for spouse.
That's why I'm sent to your noble house."

Mother Liu thanked the messenger,
But said she could not order her

Who'd made a vow, to break her word.
By Lan-zhi's brother this was heard;
As it troubled his worldly mind,
He spoke to Lan-zhi words unkind.
"Why don't you, sister, think it o'er?
You left then an official's door;
Now you may marry a noble son;
Good luck comes when bad luck is done.
If you refuse this honour great,
I know not what will be your fate."

Lan-zhi replied, raising her head,
"Brother, it's right what you have said.
I left you once to be a spouse;
Sent back, again I'm in your house.
So I'm at your disposal now.
Can I do what you don't allow?
Though I vowed to my husband dear,
We cannot meet again, I fear.
So you may marry me at will,
My obligation I'll fulfil."

The go-between learned what they said,
To his lord's house he went ahead.
He said his errand was well done;
The lord rejoiced for his fifth son.
He found in the almanac soon
The auspicious date of that moon.
He said to his subordinate,
"The thirtieth day is the best date.
That is only three days ahead.
Arrange the marriage in my stead."

The lord's order was given loud;
People bustled like floating cloud.
They painted with bird designs the boat
And with dragons the flags afloat.
A golden cab with wheels trimmed with jade
And golden saddles for steeds were made.

Three thousand strings of coins were sent
And silks to the bride with compliment.
Delicacies from land and sea
Were brought by two corteges or three.

Mother Liu told her daughter, "Word
Comes from the governor have you heard?
Tomorrow is your wedding day.
Put yourself in bridal array.
Make your own dress ere it's too late!"
Lan-zhi sat in a pensive state.
She sobbed 'neath her handkerchief,
And streaming tears revealed her grief.
She dragged a marble-seated chair
Towards the window in despair,
In her left hand the scissors bright
And silk and satin in her right.
At noon a jacket new was made
And at dusk a robe in brocade.
Behind dark clouds the sun down crept,
Grief-stricken, she went out and wept.

Zhong-qing, at this news of his spouse,
Asks leave and starts out for her house.
After a short ride on his way,
His horse makes an anguished neigh.
This neigh is familiar to her ears;
She comes out before he appears.
She gazes afar, at a loss
What to say when he comes across.
She pats the horse when it comes nigh,
And then says with a woeful sigh,
"Alas! Since you parted with me,
What's happened we could not foresee,
Our hope cannot be realized.
On hearing this, you'll be surprised.
I was compelled by my own mother
Together with my tyrant brother

To wed another man at last.
What can we do? The die is cast."

Jiao Zhong-qing tells his former wife,
"I wish you a happier life!
The lofty rock steadfast appears;
It will stand for thousands of years.
Howe'er resistant the vine may be,
'Twill lose its toughness easily.
May you live happier day by day!
Alone to death I'll go my way."
"Why say such cruel things to me?"
To her former husband says she,
"We are compelled, both you and I.
How could I live if you should die?
E'en dead, let us together stay!
Forget not what we've said today!"
They stand long hand in hand before
They go each to his or her door.
No lovers know a sharper pain
Than to part till death joins them again.
They're willing to breathe their last breath;
A severed life is worse than death.

Jiao Zhong-qing went home full of gloom;
He went straight to his mother's room.
"Today the cold wind blows down trees;
Bitten by frost, the orchids freeze.
I fear my life will end like the tree,
Leaving you alone after me.
That's what such forebodings proclaim.
Don't lay on gods or ghosts the blame!
May you like hillside rock live long
With your four limbs both straight and strong!"

On hearing this, his mother shed
Copious tears before she said,
"As son of noble family,
A high official you should be.
How could you die for such a wife?

Don't play down on your noble life!
There's a maiden in east neighbourhood,
Beside her no one else is good.
I have wooed her to be your spouse;
Soon the reply will come to our house."
Zhong-qing retired to his empty room,
Determined not to be a bridegroom.
He sighed and glanced towards the hall,
Seeing his tragic curtain fall.

In the blue tent on her wedding day
Lan-zhi heard cows low and steeds neigh.
At dusk the ghostly twilight waned;
The guests gone, lonely she remained.
"My life," she thought, "will end today.
My soul will go, but my body stay."
She doffed her silken shoes to drown
Herself in uprolled wedding gown.
This news came to her Zhong-qing's ear;
He would not be severed from his dear.
To and fro in the yard paced he,
Then hanged himself beneath a tree.

Their families, after they died,
Buried them by the mountainside.
Pine trees were planted left and right,
And planes and cypresses on the site.
Their foliage darkens the ground;
Their branches intertwined are found.
A pair of peacocks fly above;
They are well known as birds of love.
Heads up, they sing song after song,
From night to night, and all night long.
A passer-by would stand spellbound;
A lonely widow would wake dumfound.

Men of posterity, I pray,
Do not forget that bygone day!

# SIX DYNASTIES
(281-618)


## TAO QIAN (365-427)


### Return to Nature

While young, I was not used to worldly cares,
And hills became my natural compeers,
But by mistake I fell in mundane snares
And thus entangled was for thirteen years.
A caged bird would long for wonted wood,
And fish in tanks for native pools would yearn.
Go back to till my southern fields I would
To live a rustic life why not return?
My plot of ground is but ten acres square;
My thatched cottage has eight or nine rooms.
In front I have peach trees here and plums there;
O'er back eaves willow trees and elms cast glooms.
A village can be seen in distant dark,
Where plumes of smoke rise and waft in the breeze.
In alley deep a dog is heard to bark,
And cocks crow as if o'er mulberry trees.
Into my courtyard no one should intrude,
Nor rob my private rooms of peace and leisure.
After long years of abject servitude,
Again in nature I find homely pleasure.


### Drinking Wine

Among the haunts of men I build my cot,
There's noise of wheels and hoofs, but I hear not.
How can it leave upon my mind no trace?

Secluded heart creates secluded place.
I pick fence-side chrysanthemums at will
And leisurely I see the southern hill,
Where mountain air is fresh both day and night,
And where I find home-going birds in flight.
What is the revelation at this view?
Words fail me e'en if I try to tell you.

## An Elegy for Myself

Wherever there is life, there must be death;
Sooner or later we'll breathe our last breath.
Last night we lived as men who fill their posts;
Today my name's enlisted among the ghosts.
Where is my soul that's fled far, far away?
A shrivelled form in wooden box would stay.
My children seek after their father, crying;
My friends caress my dead body, sighing.
For gain or loss I no longer care,
And right or wrong is no more my affair.
Thousands of springs and autumns pass away,
So will disgrace and glory of today.
Perchance I may regret, while living still,
I have not drunken good wine to my fill.

## BAO ZHAO

### The Mume

In midcourt there are many trees,
To the mume my admiration goes.
Why this singular favour, please?*
In defiance of frost it blows.
It has borne fruit in spite of frost

---

* Weng Xian-liang's translation versified.

And danced in wind to win the vernal morn,
While other blooms in icy blasts are lost
Or from the branches they are torn.


## XIE TIAO (464-499)


### Ascending the Three Peaks at Dusk
### and Gazing at the Capital

Like poets of bygone days
Fixing on the capital their gaze,
I see from distance high and low
Winglike tiled roofs in sunset's glow.
The coloured clouds spread like brocade,
The river calm as silver braid.
The islet's loud with birds' wild cries,
Fragrant with blooms of varied dyes.
Oh, I am going far away.
Can I not miss this merry day?
When may I come and stay again?
Tears fall like pearls of snow or rain.
So deeply I long to be back
My hair turns grey from black.


## WEI DING


### To a Blackbird at the Capital

Scenes change when we are far apart;
A burst of song strikes me to the heart.
How could you sing to those who roam
The tune they used to hear at home!*

---

* Weng Xian-liang's translation versified.

# ANONYMOUS

## A Shepherd's Song

By the side of the rill,
At the foot of the hill,
The grassland stretches 'neath the firmament tranquil.

The boundless grassland lies
Beneath the boundless skies.
When the winds blow
And grass bends low,
My sheep and cattle will emerge before your eyes.

## Song of the Western Islet

Dreaming of the mume blossoms snowing,
To Western Islet again she's going;
She'll send a sprig to northern shore
For her beloved she sees no more.
In apricot-yellow silk dress,
E'en blackbirds envy her dark tress.
Where is the Western Islet? Where?
She rows across the bridge o'er there,
Only to find shrikes wheeling low*
And through the trees at dusk winds blow.

Beneath the tree, inside the gate,
Her hair adorned, she comes to wait.
Her lover comes not to her bower;
She goes to gather lotus flower.
In south pool she plucks lotus red,
Which grows e'en high above her head.
She bows and picks some lotus seed
So green that water can't exceed.

---

* Weng Xian-liang's translation versified.

She puts some flowers in her sleeves,
Red at the core as she perceives.
He still comes not; she's ill at ease
And watches for flying wild geese.
The geese are mute just as the flower;
She goes to the top of the tower.
To bring him within sight it fails;*
All day long she stops at the rails.
In vain she leans on balustrade,
Lets fall her hands, white like jade.
She sees as she rolls up the screen
The sky and waves in vain are green.

"Our dreams are severed by the sea,
From grief nor you nor I am free.
If the south wind should know my heart,
It would not set us far apart."

## Song of Mulan

Alack, alas! alack, alas!**
She weaves and sees the shuttle pass.
You cannot hear the shuttle, why?
Its whir is drowned in her deep sigh.

"Oh, what are you thinking about?
Will you tell us? Will you speak out?"
"I have no worry on my mind,
Nor have I grief of any kind.
I read the battle roll last night;
The Khan has ordered men to fight.
The roll was written in twelve books;
My father's name was in twelve nooks.
My father has no grown-up son,
For elder brother I have none.

*&** Weng Xian-liang's translation versified.

I'll get a horse of hardy race
And serve in my old father's place."

She buys a steed at eastern fair,
A whip and saddle here or there.
She buys a bridle at the south
And metal bit for horse's mouth.

At dawn she leaves her parents by the city wall;
At dusk she reaches Yellow River shore.
All night she listens for old folks' familiar call,
But hears only the Yellow River's roar.

At dawn she leaves the Yellow River shore;
To Mountains Black she goes her way.
At night she hears old folks' familiar voice no more,
But only on north mountains Tatar horses neigh.

For miles and miles the army march along
And cross the mountain barriers as in flight.
The northern wind has chilled the watchman's gong,
Their coat of mail glistens in wintry light.
In ten years they've lost many captains strong,
But battle-hardened warriors come back in delight.

Back, they have their audience with the Khan in the
    hall,
Honours and gifts are lavished on warriors all.
The Khan asks her what she wants as a grace.
"A camel fleet to carry me to my native place."

Hearing that she has come,
Her parents hurry to meet her at city gate,
Her sister rouges her face at home,
Her younger brother kills pig and sheep to celebrate.

She opens the doors east and west
And sits on her bed for a rest.
She doffs her garb worn under fire
And wears again female attire.

Before the window she arranges her hair
And in the mirror sees her image fair.
Then she comes out to see her former mate,
Who stares at her in amazement great:
"We have marched together for twelve years,
We did not know there was a lass 'mid our compeers!"
"Both buck and doe have a lilting gait
And both their eyelids palpitate.
When side by side two rabbits go,
Who can tell the buck from the doe?"*

* Weng Xian-liang's translation versified.

# TANG DYNASTY
(618-907)


## *YU SHI-NAN (558-638)*

### The Firefly

You shed a flickering light;
Your wings are weak in flight.
Afraid to be unknown,
At night you gleam alone.


## *KONG SHAO-AN (577-?)*

### Falling Leaves

In early autumn I'm sad to see falling leaves;
They're  dreary like a roamer's heart that their fall
   grieves.
They twist and twirl as if struggling against the breeze;
I  seem to hear them cry, "We will not leave our trees."


## *WANG JI (590-644)*

### The Wineshop*

Drinking wine all day long,
I won't keep my mind sane.

---

   * Written during the war that preceded the Tang Dynasty.

Seeing the drunken throng,
Should I sober remain?

# MONK OF COLD HILL

### Long, Long the Pathway to Cold Hill

Long, long the pathway to Cold Hill;
Drear, drear the waterside so chill.
Chirp, chirp, I often hear the bird;
Mute, mute, nobody says a word.
Gust by gust winds caress my face;
Flake on flake snow covers all trace.
From day to day the sun won't shine;
From year to year no spring is mine.

# WANG BO (649-676)

### Prince Teng's Pavilion

By riverside* towers Prince Teng's Pavilion proud,
But gone are cabs with ringing bells and stirring
    strains.
At dawn its painted beams bar the south-flying cloud;
At dusk its curtains furled face western mountains'
    rains.
Free clouds cast shadows in the pool from day to day;
The world and seasons change beneath the changing
    sky.
Where is the prince who in this pavilion did stay?
Beyond the balustrade the silent river rolls by.

---

* By the side of the Gan River at present-day Nanchang, Jiangxi
Province.

## Farewell to Prefect Du

You'll leave the town walled far and wide
For mist-veiled land by riverside.
I feel on parting sad and drear,
For both of us are strangers here.
If you've a friend who knows your heart,
Distance can't keep you two apart.
At crossroads where we bid adieu,
Do not shed tears as women do!

## YANG JIONG (650-695?)

### I Would Rather Fight

The beacon fire shines o'er the capital,
My agitated mind can't be calmed down.
By royal order we leave palace hall;
Our armoured steeds besiege the Dragon Town.
Snow darkens pictures sewn on banners red;
In howling winds are mingled our drumbeats.
I'd rather fight at a hundred men's head
Than pore o'er books without performing feats.

## LUO BIN-WANG (?-684)

### The Cicada Heard in Prison

In autumn the cicada sings;
A prisoner, I'm lost in thought.
I cannot bear to see its dark wings,
Which to my head white hair have brought.
Heavy with dew, it cannot fly;
Drowned in the wind, its song's not heard.

No one believes its spirit high.
Who could express my grief in word?

## WEI CHENG-QING (?-707)

### Southbound, I Part from
### My Younger Brother

On and on flows the River Long;
Deep and deep grows our grief to part.
The flowers fall mute all along
As if they too were sad at heart.

## SONG ZHI-WEN (656-712)

### Crossing the River Han*

Exiled, I longed for news none bring,
From the long winter to late spring.
Now nearing home, timid I grow,
I dare not ask what I would know.

## SHEN QUAN-QI (656?-714)

### The Garrison at Yellow Dragon Town

Stationed at Yellow Dragon Town, the men
Have never been relieved year after year.
At home their wives are watching the moon, when
They're staying in the camp on the frontier.
Their wives are longing for them when spring comes

---

* In present-day Hubei Province.

And can't forget their love on parting night.
Oh, who will lead our troops with flags and drums
To put the foe at Dragon Town to flight!


## HE ZHI-ZHANG (659-744)

### The Willow

The slender tree is dressed in emerald all about,
A thousand branches droop like fringes made of jade.
But do you know by whom these slim leaves are cut
    out?
The wind of early spring is sharp as scissor blade.


### Homecoming

Old, I return to the homeland I left while young,
Thinner has grown my hair, though I speak the
    same tongue.
My children, whom I meet, do not know who am I.
"Where are you from, dear sir?" they ask with
    beaming eye.


## CHEN ZI-ANG (661-702)

### On Climbing the Tower at Youzhou

Where are the great men of the past?
Where are those of future years?
The sky and earth forever last;
Here and now I alone shed tears.

## ZHANG YUE (667-730)

### My Delayed Departure for Home

My heart outruns the moon and sun;
It makes the journey not begun.
The autumn wind won't wait for me;
It arrives there where I would be.

## ZHANG JIU-LING (673-740)

### Since My Lord from Me Parted

Since my lord from me parted,
I've left unused my loom.
The moon wanes, brokenhearted,
To see my growing gloom.

## ZHANG RUO-XU (fl. 705)

### A Moonlit Night on the Spring River

In spring the river rises as high as the sea,
And with the river's rise the moon uprises bright.
She follows the rolling waves for ten thousand li,
And where the river flows, there overflows her light.

The river winds around the fragrant islet where
The blooming flowers in her light all look like snow.
You cannot tell her beams from hoar frost in the air,
Nor from white sand upon Farewell Beach below.

No dust has stained the water blending with the skies;
A lonely wheellike moon shines brilliant far and wide.

Who by the riverside first saw the moon arise?
When did the moon first see a man by riverside?

Ah, generations have come and past away;
From year to year the moons look alike, old and new.
We do not know tonight for whom she sheds her ray,
But hear the river say to its water adieu.

Away, away is sailing a single cloud white;
On Farewell Beach pine away maples green.
Where is the wanderer sailing his boat tonight?
Who, pining away, on the moonlit rails would lean?

Alas! The moon is lingering over the tower;
It should have seen the dressing table of the fair.
She rolls the curtain up and light comes in her bower;
She washes but can't wash away the moonbeams there.

She sees the moon, but her beloved is out of sight;
She'd follow it to shine on her beloved one's face.
But message-bearing swans can't fly out of moonlight,
Nor can letter-sending fish leap out of their place.

Last night he dreamed that falling flowers would not
    stay.
Alas! He can't go home, although half spring has gone.
The running water bearing spring will pass away;
The moon declining over the pool will sink anon.

The moon declining sinks into a heavy mist;
It's a long way between southern rivers and eastern
    seas.
How many can go home by moonlight who are missed?
The sinking moon sheds yearning o'er riverside trees.

# WANG WAN (fl. 712)

## Passing by the Northern Mountains

My boat goes by the green, green mountainside;
It glides over blue, blue water with ease.
The banks are pushed far back at full tide;*
A single sail seems hanging in the breeze.
The sun emerges ere night has passed away,
And spring intrudes to ring out the old year.
Who'll send my letter home without delay?
I see no northward-flying wild geese here.**

# WANG HAN (687-726)

## Starting for the Front

From cups of jade that glow with wine of grapes
    at night,
Drinking to pipa songs, we are summoned to fight.
Don't laugh if we lie drunk upon the battleground!
How many warriors ever came back safe and sound?

# WANG ZHI-HUAN (688-742)

## On the Heron Tower

The sun beyond the mountains glows;
The Yellow River seawards flows.
You can enjoy a grander sight
By climbing to a greater height.

---

* Weng Xian-liang's translation.
** Wild geese were believed to be message-bearing birds.

## Out of the Great Wall

The yellow sand rises as high as white cloud;
The lonely town is lost amid the mountains proud.
Why should the Mongol flute complain no willows
　　grow?
Beyond the Jade Gate vernal wind will never blow!

## MENG HAO-RAN (689-740)

### Spring Morning

This morn of spring in bed I'm lying,
Not to awake till birds are crying.
After one night of wind and showers,
How many are the fallen flowers!

### Mooring on the River at Jiande

My boat is moored by mist-veiled rivershore;
I'm grieved to see the setting sun no more.
On boundless plain clouds hang atop the tree;
In water clear the moon seems near to me.

## LI QI (690-751)

### An Old War Song

We climb the hill by day to watch for beacon fires
And water horses by riverside when day expires.
We strike the gong in sand-darkened land where
　　wind blows

And hear the pipa tell the Princess'* secret woes.
There is no town for miles and miles but tents in a row;
Beyond the desert there's nothing but rain and snow.
The wild geese honk from night to night, that's all
    we hear;
We see but Tatar soldiers shedding tear on tear.
'Tis said we cannot go back through the Jade-Gate
    Pass,
We'd risk our lives to follow war chariots, alas!
The dead are buried in the desert year on year,
Only to bring back grapes from over the frontier.


# WANG CHANG-LING (698-756)


## On the Frontier

The moon o'er mountain pass is still the moon of yore;
The men who went to guard the pass are now no more.
Were Flying General** still in Dragon City here,
No Tatar steed would dare to cross the north frontier.


## Sorrow of a Young Bride in Her Boudoir

Nothing in her boudoir brings sorrow to the bride;
She mounts the tower, gaily dressed, on a spring day.
Suddenly seeing willows green by the roadside,
Oh, she regrets her lord seeking fame far away!

---

\* The Princess refers to the beautiful Lady Wang Zhaojun, who
was married upon royal order to the Khan of the Tatar tribe in 33
B.C.

\*\* Flying General Li Guang (died in A.D. 125) of the Han
Dynasty was much dreaded by the Tatar tribesmen.

# WANG WEI (701-761)

## The Deer Enclosure

In pathless hills no man's in sight,
But I still hear echoing sound.
In gloomy forest peeps no light,
But sunbeams slant on mossy ground.

## The Dale of Singing Birds

I hear osmanthus blooms fall unenjoyed;
When night comes, hills dissolve into the void.
The rising moon arouses birds to sing,
Their fitful twitters fill the dale with spring.

## Parting Among the Hills

I watch you leave the hills, compeer;
At dusk I close my wicket door.
When grass turns green in spring next year,
Will you return with spring once more?

## Love Seeds

Red berries grow in southern land.
How many load in spring the trees!
Gather them till full is your hand;
They would revive fond memories.

## Blue Fields in Mist or Rain

O'er pebbles grey a blue stream glides;
Red leaves are strewn on jade hillsides.

Along the path it rains unseen;
My gown grows moist with drizzling green.

## Thinking of My Brothers on Mountain-Climbing Day

Alone, a lonely stranger in a foreign land,
I pine for kinsfolk doubly on a holiday.
I know my brothers would, with dogwood spray* in
    hand,
Climb the mountain and think of me so far away.

## A Farewell Song

The little town is quiet after morning rain;
No dust has dulled the tavern willows fresh and green.
I would ask you to drink a cup of wine again;
West of the Sunny Pass no more friends will be seen.

## Farewell to Spring

From day to day man will grow old,
So drink the cup of wine you hold!
Don't grieve o'er flowers falling here;
They'll come with spring from year to year.

# LIU SHEN-XU (fl. 723)

## A Scholar's Retreat

The pathway ends where white clouds rise;
Spring reigns as far as Blue Stream goes.

---

* A dogwood spray carried on mountain-climbing day, that is, the
ninth day of the ninth lunar month, was supposed to drive away evil
spirits.

Now and then fragrant flower flies;
Where water runs, its fragrance flows.
The pathway leads to doors oft shut;
A study's shaded by willow trees.
From dazzling sun is screened the hut;
Soft light is filtered by the breeze.


## LI BAI (701-762)


### The Moon Over Mount Brow

The crescent moon shines bright like autumn's golden
    brow;
Its deep reflection flows with limpid water blue.
I'll leave the town on Clear Stream for Three Gorges
    now.
O Moon, how I miss you when you are out of view!*


### Watching from Afar the Waterfall on Mount Lu

The sunlit Censer Peak exhales a wreath of cloud;
Like an upended stream the cataract sounds loud.
Its torrent dashes down three thousand feet from high,
As if the Silver River** fell from azure sky.


### A Trader's Wife

My forehead covered by my hair cut straight,
I played with flowers pluck'd before the gate.
On hobbyhorse you came upon the scene,
Around the well we played with mumes still green.
We lived, close neighbours on Riverside Lane,

---

* The moon was screened from view by riverside cliffs.
** The Chinese name for the Milky Way.

Carefree and innocent, we children twain.
At fourteen years when I became your bride,
I'd often turn my bashful face aside.
Hanging my head, I'd look towards the wall,
A thousand times I'd not answer your call.
At fifteen years when I composed my brows,
To mix my dust with yours were my dear vows.
Rather than break faith, you declared you'd die.
Who knew I'd live alone in a tower high?
I was sixteen when you went far away,
Passing Three Gorges studded with rocks grey,
Where ships were wrecked when spring flood ran high,
Where gibbons' wails seemed coming from the sky.
Green moss now overgrows before our door,
Your footprints, hidden, can be seen no more.
Moss can't be swept away, so thick it grows,
And leaves fall early when the west wind blows.
The yellow butterflies in autumn pass
Two by two o'er our western garden grass.
This sight would break my heart and I'm afraid,
Sitting alone, my rosy cheeks would fade.
Oh, when are you to leave the Western land?
Do not forget to let me know beforehand!
I'll walk to meet you and not call it far
To go to Long Wind Sands or where you are.


## Thoughts on a Silent Night

Before my bed a pool of light—
Can it be frost upon the ground?
Eyes raised, I see the moon so bright;
Head bent, in homesickness I'm drowned.

## Seeing Meng Hao-ran Off at Yellow Crane Tower

My friend has left the west where towers Yellow Crane
For River Town while willow down and flowers reign.
His lessening sail is lost in the boundless azure sky,
Where I see but the endless river rolling by.


## Invitation to Wine

Do you not see the Yellow River come from the sky,
Rushing into the sea and ne'er come back?
Do you not see the mirror bright in chamber high
Grieve o'er your snow-white hair that once was silken
     black?
When hopes are won, oh, drink your fill in high delight
And never leave your wine cup empty in moonlight!
Heaven has made us talents; we're not made in vain.
A thousand gold coins spent, more will turn up again.
Kill a cow, cook a sheep and let us merry be,
And drink three hundred cupfuls of wine in high glee!
Dear friends of mine,
Cheer up, cheer up!
I invite you to wine.
Do not put down your cup!
I will sing you a song, please hear,
O hear! Lend me a willing ear!
What difference will rare and costly dishes make?
I want only to get drunk and never to wake.
How many great men were forgotten through the ages?
Great drinkers are better known than sober sages.
The Prince of Poets* feasted in his palace at will,
Drank wine at ten thousand coins a cask and laughed
     his fill.
A host should not complain of money he is short;
To drink together we'd sell things of any sort.
The fur coat worth a thousand coins of gold

_____
* Cao Zhi, prince of the Kingdom of Wei (see note to Cao Zhi's
poems).

And flower-dappled horse may both be sold
To buy good wine that we may drown the woes age-old.


## Drinking Alone Under the Moon

Among the flowers from a pot of wine
I drink alone beneath the bright moonshine.
I raise my cup to invite the moon, who blends
Her light with my shadow and we're three friends.
The moon does not know how to drink her share;
In vain my shadow follows me here and there.
Together with them for the time I stay
And make merry before spring's spent away.
I sing the moon to linger with my song;
My shadow disperses as I dance along.
Sober, we three remain cheerful and gay;
Drunken, we part and each goes his way.
Our friendship will outshine all earthly love;
Next time we'll meet beyond the stars above.


## Mount Skyland Ascended in a Dream
## — A Song of Farewell

Of fairy isles seafarers speak,
'Mid dimming mist and surging waves, so hard to seek;
Of Skyland southerners are proud,
Perceivable through fleeting or dispersing cloud.
Mount Skyland threatens heaven, massed against the
　　sky,
Surpassing the Five Peaks and dwarfing Mount Red
　　Town.
Mount Heaven's Terrace, five hundred thousand feet
　　high,
Nearby to the southeast, appears to crumble down.
Longing in dreams for southern land, one night
I flew o'er Mirror Lake in moonlight.
My shadow's followed by moonbeams

Until I reach Shimmering Streams,
Where hermitage of Master Xie* can still be seen
And gibbons wail o'er rippling water green.
I put on Xie's pegged boot,
One on each foot,
And scale the mountain ladder to blue cloud.
On eastern cliff I see
The sun rise from the sea
And in midair I hear sky cock crow loud.
The footpath meanders 'mid a thousand crags in the
    vale;
I'm lured by rocks and flowers when the day turns pale.
Bears roar and dragons howl and thunders the cascade;
Deep forests quake and ridges tremble; they're afraid.
From dark, dark cloud comes rain;
On pale, pale waves mists plane.
Oh, lightning flashes
And thunder rumbles;
With stunning crashes
The mountain crumbles.
The stone gate of a fairy cavern under
Suddenly breaks asunder.
So blue, so deep, so vast appears an endless sky,
Where sun and moon shine on gold and silver terraces
    high.
Clad in the rainbow, riding on the wind,
The Lords of Clouds descend in a procession long.
Theis chariots drawn by phoenix disciplined,
And tigers playing for them a zither song,
Row upon row, like fields of hemp, immortals throng.
Suddenly my heart and soul stirred, I
Awake with long, long sighs.
I find my head on pillow lies
And fair visions have gone by.
Likewise all human joys will pass away
Just as east-flowing water of olden day.
I'll take my leave of you, not knowing for how long;

---

* Xie Ling-yun (385-433), a Jin Dynasty poet who was fond of
mountaineering and made himself special pegged boots for climbing.

I'll tend a white deer among
The grassy slopes of the green hill
So that I may ride it to famous mountains at will.
How can I stoop and bow before the men in power
And so deny myself a happy hour?

### Sitting Alone Facing Peak Jingting

All birds have flown away, so high;
A lonely cloud drifts on, so free.
Gazing at Peak Jingting, nor I
Am tired of him, nor he of me.

### Farewell to a Friend

Green mountains bar the northern sky;
White water girds the eastern town.
Here is the place to say good-bye;
You'll drift like lonely thistle down.
With floating cloud you'll float away;
Like parting day I'll part from you.
We wave as you start on your way;
Our steeds still neigh, "Adieu, adieu!"

## CUI HAO (704?-754)

### Yellow Crane Tower

The sage on yellow crane was gone amid clouds white.
To what avail is Yellow Crane Tower left here?
Once gone, the yellow crane will ne'er on earth alight;
Only white clouds still float in vain from year to year.
By sunlit river trees can be counted one by one;
On Parrot Islet sweet green grass grows fast and thick.
Where is my native land beyond the setting sun?

The mist-veiled waves of River Han make me
  homesick.


## ZHANG XU* (fl. 711)

### To a Guest in the Hills

On all things in the hills spring sheds a golden light.
Do not go back when shady rain clouds come in sight.
Even on a fine day when the sun shines bright,
Your gown will moisten in the thick of clouds white.


## CHANG JIAN (fl. 727)

### A Buddhist Retreat in a Ruined Mountain Temple

I come to an ancient temple at first light;
The lofty trees are steeped in sunbeams white.
A winding footpath leads to deep retreat,
Where Dhyana Cell is hid 'mid flowers sweet.
In mountain's aura flying birds feel pleasure;
In shaded pool the carefree mind finds leisure.
All worldly sounds are hushed here and there,
But chimes of bells still linger in the air.


## GAO SHI (706-765)

### Song of the Northern Frontier

A cloud of smoke and dust spreads o'er northeast
  frontier;

* A famous calligrapher of whom a description may be found in
Du Fu's poem "Eight Immortal Drinkers."

To fight the remnant foe our generals leave the rear.
Brave men should go no matter where beneath the sky;
The emperor bestows on them his favour high.
To the beat of drum and gong through Elm Pass they
    go,
Round Mount Stone Tablet flags serpentine row on
    row.
But urgent orders speed over the Sea of Sand;
Mount Wolf aflame with fires set by the Tatar band.
Both hills and streams are desolate on border plain;
The Tatar horsemen flurry like the wind and rain.
Half our warriors lie killed on the battleground,
While pretty girls in camp still sing and dance their
    round.
Grass withers in the desert as autumn is late;
At sunset few men guard the lonely city gate.
Imperial favour makes them hold the foemen light;
Their town is under siege, though they've fought with
    all their might.
In coats of mail they've served so long on the frontiers,
Since they left home their wives have shed streams of
    impearled tears.
In southern towns the women weep with broken heart;
In vain their men look southward, still they're far
    apart.
The northern front at stake, how can they go away?
On borders vast and desolate, how can they stay?
All day a cloud of slaughter mounts now and again;
All night the boom of gong is heard to chill the plain.
Each sees the other's sword bloodstained in the hard
    strife.
Will they care for reward when they give up their life?
Do you not know
The bitterness of fighting with the foe?
Can they forget the general sharing their weal and woe?

## CHU GUANG-XI (707-760?)

### The Fishing Bay

He comes to fish by lakeside green;
Late apricot blossoms run riot.
The pool seems shallow, for it's clean;
Fish go and leave lotus unquiet.
He waits for her by parting day;
And moors his boat at Willow Bay.

## XU AN-ZHEN

### My Neighbour's Lute

The Bear athwart the sky, the night is waxing deep,
I gaze upon the moon, too sad to fall asleep.
Suddenly from the bower I hear a lute is played,
I know it must be she, my neighbour's lovely maid.
The music sweet reminds me of her eyebrows fair;
Her fingers must be cold when lively turns the air.
But locked are her doors for the eyes indiscreet,
So I cannot see her but in the dreamland sweet.

## ZHANG WEI (711-777)

### Early Mume Blossoms

Like white-jade belt against the cold mume flowers
    look,
Beside the pathway near the bridge over a brook.
If you don't know the streamside blossoms early blow,
You would take them for last winter's unmelted snow.

## WAN CHU

### A Dancer at Dragon-Boat Festival

Don't say the Western Beauty stands without a peer!
Today Green Jade rivals Flowers we revere.
Her eyebrows take the colour of the verdant grass;
Her crimson skirt e'en pomegranate cannot surpass.
She sings a charming song and there's none but is
    charmed;
Her dance with captivating eyes makes all disarmed.
Who says the rainbow-hued threads can prolong our
    life?*
Tonight we'll give it up without an inner strife.


## LIU CHANG-QING (709-780)

### Seeking Shelter in Lotus Hill on a Snowy Night

At sunset hillside village still seems far;
Cold and deserted the thatched cottages are.
At wicket gate a dog is heard to bark;
With wind and snow I come when night is dark.


## DU FU (712-770)

### Gazing at Mount Tai

O, peak of peaks, how high it stands!
One boundless green o'erspreads two states.
A marvel done by nature's hands,

---

    * It was believed that five-coloured threads wound around the arm
on Dragon-Boat Festival, the fifth day of the fifth lunar month,
could prolong life.

O'er light and shade it dominates.
Clouds rise therefrom and lave my breast;
I strain my eyes and see birds fleet.
I must ascend the mountain's crest;
It dwarfs all peaks under my feet.


**Song of the Conscripts**

Chariots rumble
And horses grumble.
The conscripts march with bow and arrows at the waist.
Thir fathers, mothers, wives and children come in
    haste
To see them off; the bridge is shrouded in dust they've
    raised.
They clutch at the men's coats and stamp and bar the
    way;
Their grief cries loud and strikes the cloud straight,
    straightaway.
An onlooker by roadside asks an enrollee,
"The conscription is frequent," only answers he.
"Some went north at fifteen to guard the rivershore
And were sent west to till the land at forty-four.
The elder bound their young heads when they went
    away;
Just home, they're sent to the frontier though their
    hair's grey.
The field on borderland becomes a sea of blood;
The emperor's greed for land is still at high flood.
Have you not heard two hundred districts east of the
    Hua Mountain lie
Where briers and brambles grow in villages far and
    nigh?
Although stout women can wield the plough and the
    hoe,
They know not east from west where thorns and weeds
    o'ergrow.
The enemy are used to hard and stubborn fight:

Our men are driven just like dogs or fowls in flight.
You are kind to ask me.
To complain I'm not free.
In winter of this year
Conscription goes on here.
The magistrates for taxes press;
How can we pay them in distress!
If we had known sons bring no joy,
We'd have preferred girl to boy.
A daughter can be married to a neighbour, alas!
A son can only be buried under the grass!
Have you not seen
On borders green
Bleached bones since olden days unburied on the plain?
The old ghosts weep and cry, while the new ghosts
    complain;
The air is loud with screech and scream in gloomy rain."


## Spring View

On war-torn land streams flow and mountains stand;
In towns unquiet grass and weeds run riot.
Grieved o'er the years, flowers are moved to tears;
Seeing us part, birds cry with broken heart.
The beacon fire has gone higher and higher;
Words from household are worth their weight in gold.
I cannot bear to scratch my grizzling hair;
It grows too thin to hold a light hairpin.


## The Pressgang at Stone Moat Village

I seek for shelter as night falls;
A pressgang comes and presses for more.
My poor old host climbs o'er the walls;
My hostess old answers the door.
How angry is the sergeant's shout!
How pitiful the woman's plight!

I hear what she tries to speak out:
"All my three sons have gone to fight,
And one of them sent word to me;
The other two in battle slain,
He'll keep alive if he can be;
The dead can't come to life again.
Within the house no man is left
Except my grandson at the breast;
His mother now of all bereft
Cannot come out, in tatters drest.
Though I'm a woman weak and old,
I beg to follow on your heels
That I may serve at the stronghold
And cook for you the morning meals."
With night her voices fade away;
I seem to hear still sob and sigh.
At dawn I go upon my way
And only bid my host good-bye.

## Written at Random

The river's brokenhearted to see spring pass away;
Standing on fragrant islet, I ask spring to stay.
But willow downs run wild and dance with wanton
    breeze;
Peach blossoms frivolous go with the stream at ease.

## Welcome Rain on a Spring Night

Happy rain comes in time
When spring is in its prime.
With soft night breeze 'twill fall
And mutely moisten all.
Clouds darken rivershore;
Lamps brighten all the more.
Saturated at dawn,
With flowers blooms the town.

## Recapture of the Regions North and South of the Yellow River

'Tis said the Northern Gate has been recaptured
   of late;
When the news reaches my ears, my gown is wet with
   tears.
Staring at my wife's face, of grief I find no trace;
As I roll up verse books, my joy like madness looks.
Though white-haired, I would still both sing and drink
   my fill;
With verdure spring's aglow; 'tis time we homeward go.
We shall sail all the way through Three Gorges in a
   day;
Going down to Xiangyang, we'll go up to Luoyang.

## Ode to Autumn

The pearllike dewdrops wither maples in red dye;
The Gorge and Cliffs of Witch exhale dense fog
   around.
Waves of upsurging river seem to storm the sky;
Dark clouds o'er mountains touch their shadows on the
   ground.
Twice full-blown, asters blown off draw tears from the
   eye;
Once tied up, lonely boats tie up my heart homebound.
Thinking of winter robes, everywhere tailors ply;
I hear at dusk but nearby washing blocks fast pound.

## On the Heights

The wind so swift and sky so wide, apes wail and cry;
Water so clear and beach so white, birds wheel and fly.
The boundless forest sheds its leaves shower by shower;
The endless river rolls its waves hour after hour.

A thousand miles from home, I'm grieved at autumn's
  plight;
Ill now and then for years, alone I'm on this height.
Living in times so hard, at frosted hair I pine;
Cast down by poverty, I have to give up wine.

**Coming Across Li Gui-nian\* on the
Southern Shore of the Yangtze River**

How oft in princely mansions did we meet!
As oft in lordly halls I heard you sing.
The south with flowers is no longer sweet;
We chance to meet again in parting spring.

## CEN SHEN (715-770)

**Song of White Snow in Farewell to
Secretary Wu, Going Back to the Capital**

Snapping the pallid grass, the northern wind whirls
  low;
In the eighth moon the Tatar sky is filled with snow
As if the vernal breeze had come back overnight,
Adorning thousands of pear trees with blossoms white.
Flakes enter pearled blinds and wet the silken screen;
No furs of fox can warm us nor brocade quilts green.
The general cannot draw his rigid bow with ease;
E'en the commissioner in coat of mail would freeze.
A thousand feet o'er cracked wilderness ice piles,
And gloomy clouds hang sad and drear for miles and
  miles.
We drink in headquarters to our guest homeward
  bound;
With Tatar lutes, pipas and pipes the camps resound.
Snow in large flakes at dusk falls heavy on camp gate;

---

\* A disfavoured court musician.

The frozen red flag in the wind won't undulate.
At eastern gate of Wheel Tower we bid good-bye
On the snow-covered road to Heaven's Mountain high.
I watch his horse go past a bend and, lost to sight,
His track will soon be covered by the snow in flight.


**Song of Running-Horse River in Farewell
to General Feng on His Western Expedition**

Do you not see Running-Horse River flow
Along the sea of snow
And sand that's yellowed sky and earth and high and
    low?
In the ninth moon at Wheel Tower winds howl at
    night;
The river fills with boulders fallen from the height;
With howling winds they run riot as if in flight.
When grass turns yellow and plump Hunnish horses
    neigh,
West of Mount Gold dusts rise, the foe in proud array.
Our general leads his army on his westward way.
He keeps his iron armour on the whole night long;
Spears clang at midnight when his army march along,
Their faces cut by winds that blow so sharp and strong.
Both snow and sweat turn into steam on horse's mane,
Which soon on horse's back turns into ice again.
Ink freezes when the challenge's writ before campaign.
On hearing this, the foe with fear should palpitate.
Dare they cross swords with our brave men in iron
    plate?
We'll wait for news of victory at the western gate.

## LIU FANG-PING (fl. 742)

### A Moonlit Night

The moon has brightened half the house at dead of
    night;
The slanting Plough and Southern stars shed dying
    light.
I feel the warmth of air exhaled by coming spring
As through my window screen I hear the insects sing.

## YANG YU-HUAN (719-756)*

### Dancing

Silk sleeves are swaying ceaselessly with fragrance
    spread;
In autumn mist are floating lotus lilies red.
Light clouds o'er mountains high ripple with breezes
    cool;
Young willow shoots caress water of garden pool.

## YUAN JIE (719-772)

### Drinking Song on Stone Fish Lake**

On Stone Fish Lake as on Dongting I gaze my fill,
On brimming summer water as on verdant hill.
Using the vale as cup and water as wine pools,
The tipplers sit on rocks as cosy as on stools.

---

   * The beautiful mistress of Emperor Xuan Zong of the Tang
Dynasty. See Bai Ju-yi's long poem "The Everlasting Regret."
   ** The lake got its name from a fish-shaped rock. The poet stored
wine in the rock's concavities.

The wind so strong has formed great waves from day
    to day;
It can't prevent the boats from bringing wine this way.
A ladle in my hand, I sit on rocky shore;
To do away with care, all drink the wine I pour.


## ZHANG JI (fl. 753)

### Mooring Near Maple Bridge at Night

The moon goes down, crows cry under a frosty sky,
Dimly lit fishing boats 'neath maples sadly lie.
Beyond the Suzhou walls the Temple of Cold Hill
Rings bells, which reach my boat, breaking the
    midnight still.


## QIAN QI (722-780)

### To the Returning Wild Geese

Wild geese, why don't you stay there any more,
Where water's blue, sand bright and mossy shore?
The moonbeams play on twenty-five sad strings.*
Can you not bear the grief the zither brings?

---

   * Legend said that the Goddess of River Xiang by moonlight
played the twenty-five-stringed zither in mourning for her husband,
Emperor Shen, buried at the foot of the southern hill.

## JIA ZHI (718-772)

### Spring Thoughts

The yellow willows wave above, green grass below;
Peach blooms run riot and plum blossoms fragrant
   grow.
The vernal wind can never blow my grief away;
My woe increases with each lengthening spring day.


## HAN HONG (fl. 754)

### Cold-Food Day*

Nowhere in vernal town but sweet flowers fly down;
Riverside willow trees slant in the eastern breeze.
At dusk the palace sends privilege candles red
To lordly houses, where wreaths of smoke rise and
   spread.


## SIKONG SHU (720-790)

### Farewell to a Friend

Although I know that we shall meet again,
How can we bear on such a night to part?
Do you think wine and friendship can retain
Not longer than an adverse wind your heart?

---

   * Cold-Food Day marked the end of the three-day period when
Chinese families refrained from starting cooking fires at home. It
was also the season when they visited their ancestral burial mounds.

## *ZHANG ZHI-HE (730-810)*

**Tune: "A Fisherman's Song"**

In front of western hills white egrets fly up and down
Over peach-mirrored stream, where perches are full
    grown.
In my broad-brimmed blue hat
And green straw cloak, I'd fain
Go fishing, careless of the slanting wind and rain.

## *DAI SHU-LUN (732-789)*

**Tune: "Song of Flirtation"**

Borderland grass,
Borderland grass,
It withers up and men grow old, alas!
The south and north of mountains bright with snow,
For miles and miles bright moonbeams flow.
Bright is the moon,
Bright is the moon,
Men die of grief on hearing Hunnish tune.

## *LI DUAN (fl. 770)*

**The Zitherist**

How clear the golden zither rings
When her fair fingers touch its strings!
To draw attention from her lord,
Now and then she strikes a discord.

# WEI YING-WU (737-789)

### On the West Stream at Chuzhou

Alone, I like the riverside where green grass grows
And golden orioles sing amid the leafy trees.
When showers fall at dusk, the river overflows;
A lonely boat athwart the ferry floats at ease.

### Tune: "Song of Flirtation"

The Hunnish steed,
The Hunnish steed,
Far away at the foot of Mount Rouge it will feed.
Now through sand, now through snow, it will gallop
   and neigh.
Looking east, looking west, it's lost its backward way.
Its way is lost,
Its way is lost,
The boundless grassland with the setting sun's
   embossed.

# LU LUN (748?-800?)

### Grief in Autumn

As years pass by, grey grows my hair;
When autumn's come, the trees stand bare.
Perplexed, I ask the yellow leaf,
"Do you like me feel gnawed by grief?"

## LI YI (748-827)

### On Hearing a Flute at Night
### Atop the Victor's Wall

Below the beacon tower sand looks white as snow;
Beyond the Victor's Wall like frost cold moonbeams
    flow.
None knows from where a flute blows a nostalgic
    song;
All warriors lie awake homesick the whole night long.

## LYRICS FROM DUNHUANG

### Tune: "Buddhist Dancers"

On the pillow we make a thousand vows; we say
Our love will last unless green mountains rot away,
On the water can float a lump of lead,
The Yellow River dries up to the bed,

Stars can be seen in broad daylight,
The Dipper in the south shines bright.
E'en so, our love will not be done
Unless at midnight rise the sun.

### Tune: "The Magpie on a Branch"

How can I bear to hear the chattering magpie
Announce happy news on which I can't rely?
So thus I catch it live when it flies to me again
And shut it in a cage, where lonely 'twill remain.

With good intent I brought her a happy message.
Who would expect she'd shut me in a golden cage?

I wish her husband would come back soon, so that I
Might be set free and take my flight to the blue sky.


**Tune: "Silk-Washing Stream"**

After we pass the five-mile beach, the breeze stops
    blowing;
With sails unfurled, the boat seems light when we are
    rowing.
We use no scull and take our oars from water flowing,
But still the boat is going.

The water shimmers in the breeze before the eye;
As if to bid us welcome, the mountain comes nigh;
On a close look it does not move but towers high;
The boat is going by.


## *MENG JIAO (751-814)*


**Song of the Parting Son**

The thread in mother's hand —
A gown for parting son.
Sewn stitch by stitch, alas!
For fear of cold he'll stand.
Such kindness of warm sun
Can't be repaid by grass.


**Successful at the Civil Service Exam**

Gone are all my past woes! What more have I to say?
My body and my mind enjoy their fill today.
Successful; my horse runs faster in vernal breeze;
I've seen within one day all flowers on Chang'an trees.

# CUI HU (fl. 796)

## Written in a Village South of the Capital

This very day last year, oh, at this very place,
A pretty face outshone the flowers of peach trees.
I do not know today where shines the pretty face;
Only the pretty flowers smile in vernal breeze.

# RONG YU (fl. 780)

## Leaving the Lakeside Pavilion While Moving House

I love the lakeside pavilion in vernal breeze;
My sleeves are twined by twigs of weeping willow trees.
The orioles there nesting seem to know my heart;
They utter cry on cry before I part.

# ZHANG JI (768-830)

## Reply of a Chaste Wife

You know I love my husband best,
Yet two bright pearls are sent me still.
I hung them in my red silk vest,
So grateful I'm for your good will.
You see my house o'erlooking gardens and
My husband guards the place, halberd in hand.
I know your heart as noble as the sun in the skies,
But I have sworn to serve my husband all my life.
With your twin pearls I send back two tears from my
    eyes.
Would we had met before I was a wife!

## WANG JIAN (768-833?)

### Waiting for Her Husband

Waiting for him alone
Where the river goes by,
She turns into a stone
Gazing with longing eye.
Atop the hill from day to day come wind and rain;
The stone should speak to see her husband come again.

### Tune: "Song of Flirtation"

The willows stand,
The willows stand
At dusk at Ferry of White Sand.
The brimming river waves seen at the prow would
   make
The heart of merchant's young wife break.
'Twould break her heart,
'Twould break her heart,
To see at night a pair of partridges fly apart.

## HAN YU (768-824)

### Written for My Grandnephew
### at the Blue Pass

To the Celestial Court a proposal was made,
And I am banished eight thousand miles away.
To undo the misdeeds I would have given aid.
Would I have dared spare myself with powers in
   decay?
The ridge veiled in barred clouds, my home cannot be
   seen;

The Blue Pass covered by snow, my horse won't
    forward go.
You have come from afar and I know what you mean;
Not to leave my bones there where misty waters flow.


## ZHANG ZHONG-SU (769-819)


### In Reverie

By city wall wave willows slender
And roadside mulberry leaves tender.
She gathers not, basket in hand,
Still dreaming of the far-off land.


### The Pavilion of Swallows*

### I

Upstairs the dying lamp flickers with morning frost;
The lonely widow rises from her nuptial bed.
Sleepless the whole night long, in mournful thoughts
    she's lost;
The night seems endless as the boundless sky o'erhead.

---

* The Pavilion of Swallows in Pengcheng (present-day Xuzhou)
was where the fair lady Panpan, famous singer and dancer of the
Tang Dynasty, lived alone for ten years, refusing to remarry after
the death of her beloved lord, who was a friend of Zhang Zhong-su
and Bai Ju-yi.

## II

The pine before his grave is shrouded in sad smoke;
In the Swallows' Pavilion pensive she appears.
Her songs are hushed, for buried are his sword and
     cloak;
Her dancing dress has lost its perfume for ten years.


## III

She's seen wild geese from her lord's grave on backward
     way,
And now she sees the swallows come with spring again.
On flute and zither she is in no mood to play;
Buried in spider's webs and dusty they remain.


## *LIU YU-XI (772-842)*

### Reply to Bai Ju-yi, Whom I Meet for
### the First Time at a Banquet in Yangzhou

Oh, western mountains and southern streams desolate,
Where I, an exile, lived for twenty years and three!
To mourn for my departed friends I come too late;
In native land I look like human debris.
A thousand sails pass by the side of sunken ship;
Ten thousand flowers bloom ahead of injured tree.
Today I hear you chant the praise of comradeship;
I wish this cup of wine might well inspirit me.


### The Autumn Breeze

From where arose the autumn breeze?
It sends wild geese off sad and drear.

At dawn it enters courtyard trees;
The lonely one's the first to hear.


## Tune: "Bamboo-Branch Song"

Between the willows green the river flows along;
My dear one in a boat is heard to sing a song.
The west is veiled in rain, the east enjoys sunshine;
My dear one is as deep in love as day is fine.


## Tune: "Bamboo-Branch Song" (II)

The mountain's red with peach blossoms above;
The shore is washed by spring water below;
Red blossoms fade as fast as my gallant's love,
The river like my sorrow will ever flow.


## Tune: "Ripples Sifting Sand"

The sun dispels the mist and shines on river strand;
The crook is crowded with women washing gold from
    sand.
The seals of kings and lords, trinkets of ladies fair
Are taken from the sand by these women with care.


## Drinking Before Peonies in Bloom

Today I'll drink with blooms before.
Don't mind if I drink two cups more.
I am afraid lest to be told,
"Our bloom is not for you, the old!"*

---

* Weng Xian-liang's translation versified.

# BAI JU-YI (772-846)

## The White-Haired Palace Maid

The Shangyang Palace maid,
Her hair grows white, her rosy cheeks grow dark and
    fade.
The palace gate is guarded by eunuchs in green.*
How many springs have passed, immured as she has
    been!
She was first chosen for the imperial household
At the age of sixteen; now she's sixty years old.
The hundred beauties brought in with her have all
    gone,
Flickering out through long years, leaving her alone.*
She swallowed grief when she left home in days gone
    by;
They helped her into the cab, forbidding her tol cry.
Once in the palace, she would be favoured, they said;
Her face was fair as lotus, her bosom like jade.*
But to the emperor she could never come nigh;
The Lady Yang had cast on her a jealous eye.*
She was consigned to Shangyang Palace full of gloom,
To pass her remaining days in a lonely room.
In empty chamber long seemed each autumnal night;
Sleepless in bed, it seemed she'd never see daylight.
Dim, dim the lamplight throws her shadow on the
    walls;
Shower by shower on her window chill rain falls.
Spring days drag slow;
She sits alone to see light won't be dim and low.
She's tired to hear the palace orioles sing and sing,
Too old to envy pairs of swallows on the wing.
Silent, she sees the birds appear and disappear
And counts nor springs nor autumns coming year by
    year.
Watching the moon o'er palace again and again,

* Yang Xian-yi's translation versified.

Four hundred times and more she's seen it wax and
 wane.*
Today the oldest honourable maid of all,
She is entitled Secretary of Palace Hall.
Her gown is tightly fitted, her shoes like pointed prows;
With dark pencil she draws long, slender brows.*
Seeing her, people outside would e'en laugh with tears,
For her old-fashioned dress has been out of date for
 years.
The Shangyang maid, to suffer is her privilege;
She suffered while still young, she suffers in old age.
Do you not know a satire spread in days gone by?
Today for white-haired Shangyang Palace maid we'll
 sigh!


## The Old Charcoal Seller*

What's the old man's affair?
He cuts the wood in southern hills and fires his ware.
His face is grimed with smoke and streaked with ash and
 dust,
His temples grizzled and his fingers all turned black.
The money made by selling charcoal is not just
Enough for food and clothing for his mouth and back.
Although his coat is thin, he hopes winter will set in,
For weather cold will keep up the charcoal's good price.
At night a foot of snow falls outside the city walls;
At dawn his charcoal cart crushes ruts in the ice.
The sun is high, the ox tired out and hungry he,
Outside the southern gate in snow and slush they rest.
Two riders canter up; alas! Who can they be?
Two palace heralds in the yellow jackets dressed.
Decree in hand, which is imperial order, one says;
They turn the cart about and at the ox they shout.
A cartload of charcoal a thousand catties weights;
They drive the cart away. What dare the old man say!

---

 * Yang Xian-yi's translation versified.

Ten feet of silk and twenty feet of gauze deep red—
That is the payment they fasten to the ox's head.


## The Everlasting Regret

The beauty-loving monarch longed year after year
To find a beautiful lady without peer.
A maiden of the Yangs* to womanhood just grown,
In inner chambers bred, to the world was unknown.
Endowed with natural beauty too hard to hide,
One day she stood selected for the monarch's side.
Turning her head, she smiled so sweet and full of grace
That she outshone in six palaces the fairest face.
She bathed in glassy water of warm-fountain pool,
Which laved and smoothed her creamy skin when spring
    was cool.
Upborne by her attendants, she rose too faint to move,
And this was when she first received the monarch's
    love.
Flowerlike face and cloudlike hair, golden-headdressed,
In lotus-flower curtain she spent the night blessed.
She slept till sun rose high, for the blessed night was
    short;
From then on the monarch held no longer morning
    court.
In revels as in feasts she shared her lord's delight,
His companion on trips and his mistress at night.
In inner palace dwelt three thousand ladies fair;
On her alone was lavished royal love and care.
Her beauty served the night when dressed in Golden
    Bower
Or drunk with wine and spring at banquet in Jade
    Tower.
All her sisters and brothers received rank and fief
And honours showered on her household, to the grief
Of the fathers and mothers who'd rather give birth
To a fair maiden than any son on earth.
The lofty palace towered high into blue cloud;

* Yang Yu-huan (719-756) was the favourite mistress of Emperor
Xuan Zong (r. 725-768) of the Tang Dynasty.

With wind-borne music so divine the air was loud.
Seeing slow dance and hearing fluted or stringed song,
The emperor was never tired the whole day long.

But rebels* beat their war drums, making the earth
      quake
And "Song of Rainbow Skirt and Coat of Feathers"
      break.
A cloud of dust was raised o'er city walls nine-fold;
Thousands of chariots and horsemen southwestward
      rolled.
Imperial flags moved slowly now and halted then,
And thirty miles from Western Gate they stopped again.
Six armies would not march — what could be done?
      — with speed
Until the Lady Yang was killed before the steed.
None would pick up her hairpin fallen to the ground
Or golden bird and comb with which her head was
      crowned.
The monarch could not save her and hid his face in
      fear;
Turning his head, he saw her blood mix with his tear.
The yellow dust spread wide, the wind blew desolate;
A serpentine plank path led to cloud-capped Sword
      Gate.
Below the Eyebrow Mountains wayfarers were few;
In fading sunlight royal standards lost their hue.
On western waters blue and western mountains green
The monarch's heart was daily gnawed by sorrow keen.
The moon viewed from his tent shed a soul-searing
      light;
The bells heard in night rain made a heart-rending
      sound.

Suddenly turned the tide. Returning from his flight,
The monarch could not tear himself away from the
      ground

---

* The revolt broke out in 755 and forced the emperor to flee from
the capital.

Where 'mid the clods beneath the slope he couldn't
　forget
The fair-faced Lady Yang, who was unfairly slain.
He looked at ministers, with tears his robe was wet;
They rode east to the capital, but with loose rein.
Back, he found her pond and garden in the old place,
With lotus in the lake and willows by the hall.
Willow leaves like her brows and lotus like her face;
At the sight of all these, how could his tears not fall
Or when in vernal breeze were peach and plum
　full-blown
Or when in autumn rain parasol leaves were shed?
In western as in southern court was grass o'ergrown;
With fallen leaves unswept the marble steps turned red.
Actors, although still young, began to have hair grey;
Eunuchs and waiting maids looked old in palace deep.
Fireflies flitting the hall, mutely he pined away;
The lonely lampwick burned out; still he could not
　sleep.
Slowly beat drums and rang bells; night began to grow
　long;
Bright shone the Milky Way; daybreak seemed to come
　late.
The lovebird tiles grew chilly with hoar frost so strong,
And his kingfisher quilt was cold, not shared by a
　mate.
One long, long year the dead and the living were
　parted;
Her soul came not in dreams to see the brokenhearted.

A Taoist sorcerer came to the palace door,
Skilled to summon the spirit from the other shore.
Moved by the monarch's yearning for the departed fair,
He was ordered to seek for her everywhere.
Borne on the air, like flash of lightning he flew;
In heaven and on earth he searched through and
　through.
Up to the azure vault and down to deepest place,
Nor above nor below could he e'er find her trace.

He learned that on the sea were fairy mountains proud
That now appeared, now disappeared amid the cloud
Of rainbow colours where rose magnificent bowers
And dwelt so many fairies as graceful as flowers.
Among them was a queen whose name was Ever True;
Her snow-white skin and sweet face might afford a
    clue.
Knocking at western gate of palace hall, he bade
The porter fair to inform the queen's waiting maid.
When she heard there came the monarch's embassy,
The queen was startled out of dreams in her canopy.
Pushing aside the pillow, she rose and got dressed,
Passing through silver screen and pearl shade to meet
    the guest.
Her cloudlike hair awry, not full awake at all,
Her flowery cap slanted, she came into the hall.
The wind blew up her fairy sleeves and made them float
As if she danced the "Rainbow Skirt and Feathered
    Coat."
Her jade-white face crisscrossed with tears in lonely
    world
Like a spray of pear blossoms in spring rain impearled.
She bade him thank her lord, lovesick and
    brokenhearted;
They knew nothing of each other after they parted.
Love and happiness long ended within palace walls;
Days and months appeared long in the fairyland halls.
Turning her head and fixing on the earth her gaze,
She saw no capital 'mid clouds of dust and haze.
To show her love was deep, she took out keepsakes old
For him to carry back, hairpin and case of gold.
Keeping one side of the case and one wing of the pin,
She sent to her dear lord the other half of the twin.
"If our two hearts as firm as the gold should remain,
In heaven or on earth we'll sometime meet again."
At parting she confided to the messenger
A secret vow known only to her lord and her.
On seventh day of seventh moon when none was near,
At midnight in Long Life Hall he whispered in her ear,

"On high, we'd be two lovebirds flying wing to wing;
On earth, two trees with branches twined from spring
   to spring."
The boundless sky and endless earth may pass away,
But this vow unfulfilled will be regretted for aye.


## Song of a Pipa Player

One night by riverside I bade a friend good-bye;
In maple leaves and rushes autumn seemed to sigh.
My friend and I dismounted and came into the boat;
We wished to drink but there was no music afloat.
Without flute songs we drank our cups with heavy
   heart;
The moonbeams blent with water when we were to
   part.
Suddenly o'er the stream we heard a pipa sound;
I forgot to go home and the guest stood spellbound.
We followed where the music led to find the player,
But heard the pipa stop and no music in the air.
We moved our boat beside the player's to invite
Her to drink at replenished feast by lamplight.
Again we called and urged her to appear until
She came, her face half hid behind a pipa still.
She turned the pegs and tested twice or thrice each
   string;
Before a tune was played we heard her feelings sing.
Then note on note she struck with pathos deep and
   strong;
It seemed to say she'd missed her dreams all her life
   long.
Head bent, she played with unpremeditated art
On and on to pour out her overflowing heart.
She lightly plucked, slowly stroked and twanged loud
The song of "Green Waist" after that of "Rainbow
   Cloud."
The thick strings loudly thrummed like the pattering
   rain;

The fine strings softly tinkled in murmuring strain.
When mingling loud and soft notes were together
    played,
'Twas like large and small pearls dropping on plate of
    jade.
Now clear like orioles warbling in flowery land,
Then sobbing like a stream running along the sand.
But the stream seemed so cold as to tighten the string;
From tightened strings no more sound could be heard
    to ring.
Still we heard hidden grief and vague regret concealed;
Music expressed then far less than silence revealed.
Suddenly we heard water burst a silver jar,
The clash of spears and sabres coming from afar.
She made a central sweep when the music was ending;
The four strings made one sound, as of silk one is
    rending.
Silence reigned left and right of the boat, east and west;
We saw but autumn moon white in the river's breast.

She slid the plectrum pensively between the strings,
Smoothed out her dress and rose with a composed
    mien.
"I spent," she said, "in capital my early springs,
Where at the foot of Mount of Toads my home had
    been.
At thirteen I learned on the pipa how to play,
And my name was among the primas of the day.
My skill the admiration of the masters won,
And my beauty was envied by deserted fair one.
The gallant young men vied to shower gifts on me;
One tune played, countless silk rolls were given with
    glee.
Beating time, I let silver comb and pin drop down,
And spilt-out wine oft stained my blood-red silken
    gown.
From year to year I laughed my joyous life away
On moonlit autumn night or windy vernal day.
My younger brother left for war, and died my maid;

Days passed, nights came, and my beauty began to
    fade.
Fewer and fewer were cabs and steeds at my door;
I married a smug merchant when my prime was o'er.
The merchant cared for money much more than for
    me;
One month ago he went away to purchase tea,
Leaving his lonely wife alone in empty boat;
Shrouded in moonlight, on the cold river I float.
Deep in the night I dreamed of happy bygone years
And woke to find my rouged face crisscrossed with
    tears."

Listening to her sad music, I sighed with pain;
Hearing her story, I sighed again and again.
"Both of us in misfortune go from shore to shore.
Meeting now, need we have known each other before?
I was banished from the capital last year
To live degraded and ill in this city here.
The city's too remote to know melodious song,
So I have never heard music the whole year long.
I dwell by riverbank on low and damp ground
In a house yellow reeds and stunted bamboos surround.
What is here to be heard from daybreak till nightfall
But gibbons' cry and cuckoos' homeward-going call?
By blooming riverside and under autumn moon
I've often taken wine up and drunk it alone.
Of course I've mountain songs and village pipes to
    hear,
But they are crude and strident and grate on the ear.
Listening to you playing on pipa tonight,
With your music divine e'en my hearing seems bright.
Will you sit down and play for us a tune once more?
I'll write for you an ode to the pipa I adore."
Touched by what I said, the player stood for long,
Then sat down, tore at strings and played another song.
So sad, so drear, so different, it moved us deep;
All those who heard it hid the face and began to weep.

Of all the company at table who wept most?
It was none other than the exiled blue-robed host.


## A Flower in the Haze

In bloom, she's not a flower;
Hazy, she's not a haze.
She comes at midnight hour;
She goes with starry rays.
She comes like vernal dreams that cannot stay
And goes like morning clouds that melt away.


## The Last Look at the Peonies at Night

I'm saddened by the courtyard peonies brilliant red;
At dusk but two of them are left and withered.
I am afraid they can't survive the morning blast;*
By lantern light I take a look, the long, long last.


## The Pavilion of Swallows**

*After Zhang Zhong-su's poems, using the same rhyme
scheme.*

## (I)

Her room is drowned in moonlight and the screen in
    frost;
The quilt grows cold with dying lamp; she makes her
    bed.
The moonlit night in which Swallows' Pavilion's lost
Lengthens since autumn came for one who mourns the
    dead.

---

* Weng Xian-liang's translation versified.
** See Zhang-Zhong-su's "Pavilion of Swallows."

**(II)**

Her silken dress with golden flowers fades like smoke;
She tries to put it on, but soon she melts in tears.
Since she's no longer danced to the air of "Rainbow
    Cloak,"
It's been stored in the chest for ten long years.

**(III)**

Some friends come back from ancient capital and say
They've visited the grave of her dear lord again.
The graveyard poplar white grows high as pillar grey.
How can her rosy face still beautiful remain!

### Sunset and Moonrise on the River

The last departing rays pave their way on the river;
Half its waves turn red and all the others shiver.
How I pity the third night of the ninth month, alas!
The moon looks like a bow, dewdrops like pearls on
    grass.

## LI SHEN (780-846)

### The Peasants

**(I)**

Each seed that's sown in spring,
Will make autumn yields high.
What will fertile fields bring?
Of hunger peasants die.

## (II)

At noon they hoe up weeds;
Their sweat drips on the soil.
Who knows the rice that feeds
Is the fruit of hard toil!


# LIU ZONG-YUAN (773-819)


### Fishing in Snow

From hill to hill no bird in flight,
From path to path no man in sight.
A straw-cloak'd man afloat, behold!
Is fishing snow on river cold.


### Drinking*

I fill my cup with drink divine;
It is another boring day.
First let me drink to Lord of Wine,
Who helps to drive the blues away.

One draught and different I feel;
At once the world revives anew;
The hidden hills themselves reveal;
The river takes on warming hue.

Exuberant the southern gate;
Trees raise their leafy arms so nice;
With shade their roots are saturate;
All night you hear silent advice.

So drink your fill and do not stop!
Drunk, you may lie on fragrant grass.

---

* Weng Xian-liang's translation versified.

Rich revellers in the wineshop,
What have you in your cups, alas!


## LI SHE (fl. 806-820)

### Lodging Again at the Southern Pass

I've left the capital to go far, far away,
And pass the Southern Town with mountains high and
    low.
The cold stream's water, which the city gate can't stay,
Flows all night long, murmuring about my woe.


## CUI JIAO (fl. 806-820)

### To the Maid of My Aunt*

The sons of prince and lord all try to find thy trace;
Thy scarf is wet with tears streaming down thy face.
The mansion where thou enter is deep as the sea;
Thy master from now on is a stranger to thee.


## YUAN ZHEN (779-831)

### To My Deceased Wife

One day we said for fun, "What if one of us dies?"
But now it has all come to pass before my eyes.
Your clothes nearly all have been given away;

---

* The poet loved his aunt's maid, who was later married to a rich
lord. On reading this poem, the lord sent her back to the poet.

I cannot bear to see your needlework today.
Remembering your kindness, I'm kind to your maids;
Dreaming of you, to your friends I give friendly aids.
I know death is a sorrow no one can ignore,
But a poor couple like us have more to deplore.


## At an Old Palace

Deserted now imperial bowers.
For whom still redden palace flowers?
Some white-haired chambermaids at leisure
Talk of the late emperor's* pleasure.


## Chrysanthemum

Around the cottage like Tao's** autumn flowers grow;
Along the hedge I stroll until the sun hangs low.
Not that I favour partially the chrysanthemum,
But it's the flower; after it none will come.


## Thinking of My Dear Departed***

No water's wide enough when you have crossed the sea;
No cloud is beautiful but that which crowns the peak.
I pass by flowers that fail to attract poor me
Half for your sake and half for Taoism I seek.

---

* Emperor Xuan Zong (r. 725-768) of the Tang Dynasty, who
loved the beautiful Lady Yang Yu-huan (719-756). See Bai Ju-yi's
long poem "The Everlasting Regret."
** Tao Qian (365-427) who loved the chrysanthemum.
*** The poet was heart-broken after his wife's death and would
retire from the world in accordance with the teaching of Taoism, so
he was no longer attracted by beautiful flowers.

## JIA DAO (779-843)

**My Lord's Garden***

A thousand homes are shattered; a garden's laid out;
Roses grow everywhere, but no fruit-bearing trees.
When blows the autumn wind and roses fall about,
In the thorn-choked pavilion can you sit at ease?

**A Note Left for an Absent Recluse**

I ask your lad beneath a tree.
"My master's gone for herbs," says he,
"Amid the hills I know not where,
For clouds have veiled them here and there."

## ZHANG HU (?-849)

**Swan Song**

Homesick a thousand miles away,
Shut in deep palace twenty years.
Singing the dying swan's sweet lay,
Oh, how can she hold back her tears!

## LIU ZAO

**Farther North***

Ten long, long winters in northern town I did stay;
My heart cried out for home in the south night and day.

---

\* Weng Xian-liang's translation versified.

Now as I cross the river, farther north I roam;
My heart cries out for northern town as for my home.


## HUANGFU SONG

**Tune: "Dreaming of the South"**

Out candles burned;
Dark on the screen red cannas turned.
I dreamed of mume fruit ripening on southern shore,
Of flute songs played in boat one rainy night of yore,
Of whispered farewell lost
In running stream below the bridge beside the post.


## ZHU QING-YU (fl. 826)

**To an Examiner on the Eve of Examination***

Last night red candles burned bright in the bridal
     room;
At dawn she'll kowtow to new parents with the groom.
She whispers to him after touching up her face:
"Have I painted my brows with fashionable grace?"

* The poet asks the examiner whether his work is up
to the standard of the civil service examination.

# LI HE (790-816)

## Twenty-three Horse Poems*

### (I)

A string of coins upon his back, noble and proud,
His hoofs silvery white as though born to trot in cloud.
But where's the whip of gold, the saddle cloth of
    brocade?
The cloth is not yet woven; the whip not yet made.

### (IV)

This is no ordinary steed
But an incarnate star indeed.
When I tap his bony frame, what's found?
I seem to hear metallic sound.

### (V)

The desert sands look white as snow;
The crescent moon hangs like a bow.
When would the steed in golden gear
Gallop all night through autumn clear?

### (XXIII)

"I'll have elixir," Emperor Wu says,
And heaps of gold go up in purple haze.
All steeds in royal stable, ah, must die,
For none of them can run up to the sky.

---

* Weng Xian-liang's translation versified.

## XU NING (fl. 820)

### To One in Yangzhou

Your bashful face could hardly bear the weight of tear;
Your long, long brows would easily feel sorrow near.
Of all the moonlit nights on earth when people part,
Two-thirds shed light upon Yangzhou with broken
    heart.

## YONG YU-ZHI (fl. 785)

### To the Riverside Willow

Your long, long branches wave by riverside,
Your green, green leaves like wreaths of smoke afloat.
"Make ropes unbreakable of them," she sighed,
"To tie up my beloved one's parting boat!"

## XU HUN (fl. 832)

### Gazing Afar in the Evening from the West Tower of Xianyang*

On city wall I see grief spread for miles and miles
O'er reeds and willow trees as planted on flats and isles.
The sun beneath the cloud sinks o'er waterside bower;
The wind before the storm fills the mountainside
    tower.
In the wasted Qin garden only birds fly still;
'Mid yellow leaves in Han** palace cicadas shrill.

---

 * Ancient capital of the Qin Dynasty (221-207 B.C.).
 ** The Han Dynasty (206 B.C.-A.D.220).

O wayfarer, don't ask about the days gone by!
Coming from east, I hear only the river sigh.


## DU MU (803-852)


### Ruined Splendour*

Rank grasses grow, Six Dynasties** splendour's no
   more.
The sky is lightly blue and clouds free as of yore.
Birds come and go into the gloom of wooded hills,
And songs and wails alike merge in murmuring rills.
Like countless window curtains falls late autumn rain,
High towers steeped in sunset, wind and flute's refrain.
Oh, how I miss the lakeside sage*** of bygone days!
I see but ancient trees loom ragged in the haze.


### Spring Abides Not****

Spring days half gone to the year's end amount,
For all the other seasons do not count.
I drink to flowers loath to say adieu
And feel e'en wine would taste like winter brew.
I am distressed after the parting cup
The broom will sweep all fallen petals up.
From year to year thus life will pass away
Alas! There's no one who its course can stay!

---

* Weng Xian-liang's translation versified.
** The Six Southern Dynasties (221-280; 317-589).
*** Fan Li, who retired at the zenith of his political career
after the Kingdom of Yue conquered the Kingdom of Wu in 473
B.C.
**** Weng Xian-liang's translation versified.

## Moored on River Qinhuai*

Cold water veiled in mist and shores in dim moonlight,
I moor on River Qinhuai near wineshops at night,
Where songstress knowing not the grief of conquered
    land,
Still sings the songs composed by a captive ruler's
    hand.**

## Parting

Deep, deep our love, too deep to show.
Deep, deep we drink; silent we grow.
The candle grieves to see us part;
It melts in tears with burnt-out heart.

## The Day of Mourning for the Dead***

The day of mourning for the dead it's raining hard;
My heart is broken on my way to the graveyard.
Where can I find a wineshop to drown my sad hours?
A herdboy points to cots amid apricot flowers.

## *YONG TAO (805-?)*

## The Bridge of Love's End

Why should this bridge be called Love's End,
Since love without an end will last?

* In present-day Nanjing, ancient capital of the Chen Dynasty
(557-589).
** The last ruler of Chen was taken captive in 589.
*** The fourth or fifth day of April, when Chinese people used to
visit their ancestral burial mounds.

Plant willow trees for parting friend;
Your longing for him will stand fast.*


## LI CHEN ET AL. **

**To a Waterfall**

You are not tired while passing o'er a thousand crags;
I can see from afar your source in sky-high caves.
You cannot be retained by brooks or creeks or jags;
At last you will return among the ocean waves.


## WEN TING-YUN (813-870)

**Tune: "Buddhist Dancers"**

See light and shade upon her eyebrows' double peaks
And cloud-like hair overshadow her snow-white cheeks.
Idly she rises to pencil her brows;
Slowly she makes up, feeling still the drowse.

In mirrors back and front she's eying,
Her face with blooms in beauty vying.
On broidered silken vest she wears
There're golden partridges in pairs.


**Tune: "Song of Water Clock at Night"**

The tearful candle red
And fragrant censer spread
Within the painted bower a gloomy autumn light.

---

* The last two lines were rewritten by the versifier.
** The first two lines were written by a monk and the last two by
Li Chen, Emperor Xuan Zong of the Tang Dynasty.

Worn eyebrows pencilled
And hair dishevelled,
She feels her quilt the colder and longer the night.

The lonely withered trees
And midnight rain and breeze
Don't care about her bitter parting sorrow.
Leaf on leaf without grief,
Drop by drop without stop,
They fall on vacant steps until the morrow.


**Tune: "Dreaming of the South"**

After dressing my hair,
Alone I climb the stair.
On the railings I lean
To view the river scene.
A thousand sails pass by,
But not the one for which wait I.
The slanting sun sheds sympathetic ray;
The carefree river carries it away.
My heart breaks at the sight
Of the islet with duckweed white.*


## CHEN TAO (812-885)


### The Riverside Battleground

They would lay down their lives to wipe away the
    Huns;
They've bit the dust, five thousand sable-clad brave
    ones.
Alas! Their bones lie on riverside battleground,
But in dreams of their wives they still seem safe and
    sound.

---

* Place where people used to bid farewell.

# LI SHANG-YIN (812-858)

### The Sad Zither

Why should the zither sad have fifty strings?
Each string, each strain evokes but vanished springs:
Dim morning dream to be a butterfly;
Amorous heart poured out in cuckoo's cry.
In moonlit pearls see tears in mermaid's eyes;
From sunburnt emerald let vapour rise.
Such feeling cannot be recalled again;
It seemed long lost e'en when it was felt then.

### On the Plain of Tombs*

At dusk my heart is filled with gloom;
I drive my cab to ancient tomb.
The setting sun appears sublime,
But O! 'Tis near its dying time.

### Two Poems to One Unnamed

### (I)

You said you'd come, but you are gone and left no
    trace;
I wake to hear in moonlit tower the fifth watch bell.
In dream my cry couldn't call you back from distant
    place;
In haste with ink unthickened I cannot write well.
The candlelight illumines half our broidered bed;
The smell of musk still faintly sweetens lotus screen.

---

* The Merrymaking Plain was situated to the south of the capital
(present-day Xi'an), where the tombs of five emperors of the Han
Dynasty (206 B.C.-A.D.220) were.

Beyond my reach the far-off fairy mountains spread,
But you're still farther off than fairy mountains green.

**(II)**

The rustling eastern wind came with a drizzle light,
And thunder faintly rolled beyond the lotus pool.
When doors were locked and incense burned, I came at
    night
And went at dawn when windlass pulled up water
    cool.*
You peeped at me first from behind a curtained bower;
I'm left at last with but the cushion of a dame.
Let my desire not bloom and vie with vernal flower!
For inch by inch my heart is consumed by the flame.


**To One Unnamed**

It's difficult for us to meet and hard to part;
The east wind is too weak to revive flowers dead.
Spring silkworm till its death spins silk from lovesick
    heart,
And candles but when burned up have no tears to shed.
At dawn I'm grieved to think your mirrored hair turns
    grey;
At night you would feel cold while I croon by
    moonlight.
To the three fairy hills it is not a long way.
Would the blue birds oft fly to see you on the height!

---

\* The poet had a tryst with an unnamed lover.

## LI QUN-YU (813-860)

### To a Deserted Lover

Your literary fame was once loved best;
Your muse then came in dreams to lovebirds' nest.
We cannot rule o'er fickle cloud or shower,
So let it water any thirsting flower!*

## CUI JUE (fl. 847-850)

### Elegy on Li Shang-yin

In vain you could have soared to the azure sky;
Before you could fulfil your ambition you die.
The birds bewail with fallen flower: "Where are you?"
The phoenix won't alight on dead tree or bamboo.
A horse'd be crippled if not trained by riders good;
The lutist broke his lute for one who understood.
In nether world not sun or moon or stars in sight,
But you're the brightest star in the eternal night.

## ZHAO JIA (fl. 842)

### On the Riverside Tower

Alone I mount the Riverside Tower and sigh
To see the moonbeams blend with waves and waves
   with sky.
Last year I came to view the moon with my compeers.
But where are they, now that the scene is like last year's?

---

* Rewritten by the versifier.

## CAO YE (816-875)

### The Rats in the Public Granary

The rats in the public granary so fatted grow,
When they see man come in, they do not run away.
The soldiers not provided, the people hungry go.
Who allows them to eat so much from day to day?


## LUO YIN (833-909)

### To a Singing Girl

Drunken, we parted here more than ten years ago.
Now again I meet you as beautiful as then.
You are not married and my fame remains still low;
Maybe we are not equal to all other men.


### For Myself

Sing when you're happy and from worries keep away!
How can we bear so much regret and so much sorrow?
When you have wine to drink, oh, drink your fill today!
Should sorrow come, alas! Tell it to come tomorrow!


### To the Parrot

Do not complain of golden cage and wings cut short;
The southern land is far warmer than the northwest.*
Don't clearly speak, if you listen to my exhort!
You can't be free if clearly your complaint's expressed.

---

\* The poet went from the northwest to the south just as the parrot did.

**Snow**

All say that snow forebodes a bumper year.
What if it should arouse less joy than fear?
There are poor people in the capital
Who are afraid a bumper snow will fall.


## WEI ZHUANG (836-910)


**Tune: "Song of a Lady's Crown"**

**(I)**

The seventeenth of fourth month comes anew.
It was this day last year
I parted from you.
Holding back tear on tear,
Bashfully you pretended to bow
And drew together half your brow.

Not knowing that my heart is broken,
I follow you in dreams unwoken.
None knows how sad am I
But the moon in the sky.

**(II)**

Last night at middle hour
I dreamed of you who whispered on my pillow,
Your face still fair as peach-tree flower,
Your downcast brows like leaves of willow.

Half shy, half glad,
You'd go away but stop to stay.
I woke to find the dream so sad,
A grief not to allay.

## HUANG CHAO (?-884)*

**To the Chrysanthemum**

In soughing western wind you blossom far and
    nigh;
Your fragrance is too cold to invite butterfly.
Some day if I as Lord of Spring come into power,
I'll order you to bloom together with peach flower.

**The Chrysanthemum**

When autumn comes, Mountain-Climbing Day** is
    nigh;
My flower blows when others' season terminates.
All o'er the capital my fragrance rises sky high;
You'll see the city clad in golden armour plates.

## NIE YI-ZHONG (837-884)

**Poor Peasants**

Up in old fields the fathers toil;
Down in new fields the sons break soil.
The corn in sixth moon still in blade,
Government granaries are made.

---

* Huang Chao was the leader of the peasant uprising at the
end of the Tang Dynasty (618-907).
** The ninth day of the ninth lunar month.

# ZHANG JIE (837-?)

## The Pit Where Emperor Qin* Burned the Classics

Smoke of burnt classics gone up with the empire's fall,
Fortress and rivers could not guard the capital.
Before the pit turned cold, eastern rebellion spread;
The leaders of revolt were not scholars well read.

# CAO SONG (fl. 860)

## A Year of War

The lakeside country has become a battleground.
How can the peasants and woodmen live all around?
I pray you not to talk about the glories vain;
A victor's fame is built on bones of soldiers slain.

# CUI DAO-RONG (?-900)

## A Cloak of Spring

I try to cut for him a cloak of spring;
My scissors breathe the cold still lingering.
Far colder is the far-off garrison town.
How can he not expect a warrior's gown!

---

* The First Emperor of the Qin Dynasty ordered all classics
burned and 460 scholars buried alive in 213 B.C.

## JIN CHANG-XU

**A Complaint in Spring**

Drive orioles off the tree;
Their songs awake poor me
From dreaming of my dear
Far off on the frontier.


## WANG JIA (851-?)

**After the Rain**

Before the rain I still see blooming flowers;
Only green leaves are left after the showers.
Over the wall pass butterflies and bees;
I wonder whether spring's in next-door trees.


## ZHANG BI (fl. 870)

**To My Love**

When you were gone, in my dream I lingered you know
     where.
The courtyard seemed the same with zigzag rails
     around.
Only the sympathetic moon was shining there
For me alone on flowers fallen on the ground.

# ANONYMOUS

## The Golden Dress

Love not your golden dress, I pray,
More than your youthful golden hours.
Gather sweet blossoms while you may
And not the twig devoid of flowers!

# FIVE DYNASTIES
(908-960)


## *NIU XI-JI (?-925)*


### Tune: "Mountain Hawthorn"*

Spring hills are casting off their misty veil.
The sky is lightening, the stars turn pale.
The parting moon vignettes a face in tears.
This dewy morn's the end of happy years.

Much has been said,
More's left unsaid.
She says again when round she turns her head,
"If you've this green silk skirt in mind,
To green grass you'll ne'er be unkind."


## *OUYANG JIONG (895-971)*


### Tune: "Song of the Southern Country"

The sandy rivershores extend far, far away.
The clouds are gilt by slanting sun on backward way.
By waterside the peacocks preen
Their tails gold-green;
Though startled, they won't stir when passers-by are
    seen.

---

\* Weng Xian-liang's translation versified.

# GU XIONG (fl. 928)

## Tune: "Telling of Innermost Feeling"

Having deserted me,
Where hast thou gone from night to night?
No news of thee,
My scented chamber's closed tight.
My eyebrows knit,
The moon about to set,
How can I bear to think of it!
I loathe this lonely coverlet.
If thou exchanged thy heart for mine,
Then thou wouldst know how deep for thee I pine.

# LU QIAN-YI

## Tune: "Immortal at the River"

All doors are double-locked; the garden waste is still.
Painted windows face the autumn sky, so sad and chill.
The royal flag has gone and left no trace; no flute is
    played
In bowers of jade,
Gone with the wind its broken tune.

The mist-veiled moon
Knows not the change of the world; it would peep
At dead of night into the palace deep.
In the wild pool red lotus blooms still stand;
They grieve in secret for the conquered land.
On fragrant petals dewdrops weep.

## LI XUN (855-930)

### Tune: "Cloud Over Mount Witch"*

The ancient shrine still clings to the evergreen heights;
The wanton palace still lies there where waters wind.
The beauty's bower locked 'mid nature's delights,
Ghosts of romance and grandeur haunt my mind.

Each morning rosy clouds bring promise vain of bliss;
Each spring fresh buds awaken hopes of sweet fruition.
Why must these wailing monkeys come to me amiss?
A lonely trip's already a punition!

### Tune: "Song of the Southern Country"

A skiff goes along
The lotus pond.
The sleeping lovebirds start at the oarswomen's song.
Perfumed girls lean upon each other making fun
And vie to be the fairest one.
They take round lotus leaves to shun
The setting sun.

## FENG YAN-SI (903-960)

### Tune: "Butterflies Lingering Over Flowers"

Where have you gone like cloud from day to day,
Forgetting to come homeward way?

---

* Weng Xian-liang's translation versified. It was fabled that the
king of Chu had a tryst with the Goddess of Mount Witch, who
would come out in the morning in the form of a cloud and in the
evening in the form of a shower over Mount Witch, the highest peak
along the Yangtze River.

Don't you know spring's grown old and late?
Flowers and grass by roadside teem on Cold-Food Day.
Under whose tree's your scented cab and at whose gate?

Alone on balcony, with tearful eyes I query
A pair of returning swallows, dreary,
Whether they have met you on the pathway.
Spring sorrow's running wild like willow down, it seems;
Nowhere can I find you, e'en in my lonely dreams.


## Tune: "Homage at the Golden Gate"

The breeze begins to blow,
Ruffling a pool of spring water below.
Crushing pink apricot petals in hand, I play
With a pair of lovebirds on the fragrant pathway.

Watching duck fight, alone on the railings I lean
Till slants upon my head my hairpin of jade green.
Waiting for you the whole day long wears out my eyes;
Raising my head, I'm glad to hear magpies.*


## Tune: "Song of the Southern Country"

The raindrops glisten on the undulating grass,
With which my sorrow grows from year to year, alas!
In mist-veiled bower I have so much to regret
And never to forget.
The mirror and the quilt for a couple would make
My lonely heart break.

In dreams my soul may roam wherever it is led;
I wake to find the catkins o'er my broidered bed.
My fickle lover will no more
Enter my half-closed door.

---

* Magpies were supposed to announce the expected arrival.

The slanting sun would wring
Two streams of tears I owe him in departing spring.

## LI JING (916-961)*

**Tune: "Silk-Washing Stream"**

The lotus flowers fade with blue-black leaves decayed;
The grievous western wind ripples the water green
As time will wrinkle faces fair. How can they bear,
Oh, to be seen!

In the fine rain she dreams of far-away frontiers;
Out of her bower wafts cold sound of flute of jade.
She leans with much regret and many, many tears
On balustrade.

## LI YU (937-978)**

**Tune: "Pure, Serene Music"**

Spring has half gone since we two parted,
I can see nothing now but brokenhearted.
Mume blossoms fall below the steps like whirling snow;
They cover me still though brushed off a while ago.

No message comes from the wild geese's song;***
In dreams you cannot come back, for the road is long.
The grief of separation is like spring grass,
Growing each day you're farther away, alas!

---

* Second ruler of Southern Tang.
** Son of Li Jing and last ruler of Southern Tang.
*** The wild geese were supposed to be messengers in ancient China.

**Tune: "Song of Picking Mulberries"**

Red blooms are driven down by the departing spring,
Dancing while lingering.
My brows are knit again,
Though I try to unknit them in the drizzling rain.

No message comes to lonely windows all the day,
The incense burned to ashes grey.
How can I from spring thoughts be free?
I try to sleep, but in my dream spring comes to me.

**Tune: "Migrant Orioles"**

The morning moon is sinking;
Few clouds are floating there;
I lean upon my pillow with no word.
E'en in my dream I'm thinking
Of the green grass so fair,
But from afar the wild geese are not heard.

Orioles no longer sing their song;
Late vernal blooms are whirling round.
In courtyard as in painted hall
Solitude reigns the whole night long.
Don't sweep away the fallen blossoms on the ground!
Leave them there till the dancer comes back from the
    ball!

**Tune: "Buddhist Dancers"**

Bright flowers bathed in thin mist and dim moonlight,
'Tis best time to steal out to see my love tonight.*
With stocking feet on fragrant steps I tread,
Holding in hand my shoes sown with gold thread.

----

* A tryst between the poet-king and the younger sister of the
queen.

We meet south of the painted hall,
And trembling in his arms I fall.
"It's hard for me to come o'er here,
So you may love your fill, my dear!"

## Tune: "Dance of the Cavalry"

A reign of forty years
O'er land and hills and streams,
My royal palace touching the celestial spheres,
My shady forest looking deep like leafy dreams.
What did I know of shields and spears?

A captive now, I'm worn away;
Thinner I grow; my hair turns grey.
Oh, how can I forget the hurried parting day
When by the band the farewell songs were played
And I shed tears before my palace maid!

## Tune: "Midnight Song"

From sorrow and regret our life cannot be free.
Why is this soul-consuming grief e'er haunting me!
I went to my lost land in dreams;
Awake, I find tears flow in streams.

Who would ascend again those towers high?
I can't forget those autumn days gone by.
Vain is the happiness of yore;
It melts like dreams and is no more.

## Tune: "The Beautiful Lady Yu"

When will there be no more autumn moon and spring
    flowers

For me who had so many memorable hours?
My attic, which last night in vernal wind did stand,
Reminds me cruelly of the lost moonlit land.

Carved balustrades and marble steps must still be there,
But rosy faces cannot be as fair.
If you ask me how much my sorrow has increased,
Just see the overbrimming river flowing east!

**Tune: "Ripples Sifting Sand"**

The curtain cannot keep out the patter of rain;
Springtime is on the wane.
In the deep of night my quilt is not coldproof.
Forgetting I am under hospitable roof,
Still in my dream I seek for pleasure vain.

Don't lean alone on railings and
Yearn for the boundless land!
To bid farewell is easier than to meet again.
With flowers fallen on the waves spring's gone away;
So has the paradise of yesterday!

**Tune: "Crows Crying at Night"**

Spring's rosy colour fades from forest flowers
Too soon, too soon.
How can they bear cold morning showers
And winds at noon?

Her rouged tears like crimson rain
Intoxicate my heart.
When shall we meet again?
As water eastward flows, so shall we part.

## Tune: "Ripples Sifting Sand"

It saddens me to think of days gone by,
With old familiar scenes in my mind's eye.
The autumn wind is blowing hard
O'er moss-grown steps in deep courtyard.
Let beaded screen hang idly unrolled at the door.
Who will come any more?

Sunk and buried my golden armour lies;
Amid o'ergrowing weeds my vigour dies.
The blooming moon is rising in the evening sky.
The palaces of jade
With marble balustrade
Are reflected in vain on the River Qinhuai.

## Tune: "Joy of Meeting"

Silent, I climb the western tower alone,
But see the hooklike moon.
The plane-trees lonesome and drear
Lock in the courtyard autumn clear.

Cut, it won't sever;
Be ruled, 'twill never.
What sorrow 'tis to part!
It's an unspeakable taste in the heart.

## Tune: "Crows Crying at Night"

Wind soughed and rain fell all night long;
Door curtains rustled like an autumn song.
The waterclock drip-dropping and the candle dying,
I lean on pillow troubled, sitting up or lying.

All are gone with the running stream;
My floating life is but a dream.
Let wine cups be my surest haunt;
On nothing else can I e'er count.

# SONG DYNASTY
(960-1279)

## LADY PISTIL (fl. 965)

### Written at the Capitulation
### of the Kingdom of Shu*

My lord erected "surrender flag" on city wall.
How could a woman living deep in palace know?
They were disarmed, one hundred forty thousand men
   in all;
Not one of them was man enough to fight the foe.

## ZHENG WEN-BAO (952-1012)

### Tune: "Willow-Branch Song"

The painted ship on vernal lake has tarried long;
Until half drunk no one will sing a farewell song.
At last the sorrow-laden ship goes on before
Through mist and rain, through wind and wave to
   southern shore.

---

  * The ruler of Shu surrendered to the first emperor of the Song
Dynasty in 965. His favourite Lady Pistil was famed for her poetry;
the emperor ordered her to write the above poem impromptu.

## *LIN BU (967-1028)*

**To the Mume Blossom**

You bloom alone when flowers fade out far and near;
You queen it over all the garden day and night.
Sparse shadows slant across the shallow water clear;
Your gloomy fragrance floats at dusk in dim moonlight.
Seeing your purity, white birds alight and peer;
Knowing your sweetness, butterflies lose their heart.
Only a lucky poet's your companion dear.
Put sandal clappers and golden goblets apart!*

## *PAN LANG (?-1009)*

**Tune: "Fountain of Wine"**

I still remember watching tidal bore;
The city poured out people on the shore.
It seemed the sea had emptied all its water here,
And thousands of drums were beating far and near.

At the crest of huge billows the swimmers did stand,
Yet dry remained red flags they held in hand.
Back, I saw in dreams the tide o'erflow the river;
Awake, I feel my heart with cold still shiver.

## *LIU YONG (987-1053)*

**Tune: "Joy of Day and Night"**

In nuptial chamber first I saw your face;
I thought we should forever share the place.

---

* Singers and drinkers are not your good companions.

The short-lived joy of love, who would believe?
Soon turned to parting that would grieve.
Now late spring has grown old and soon takes leave;
I see a riot of catkins and flowers
Fallen in showers.
I am afraid all the fine scenery
Will go away with thee.

Whom may I tell my solitude?
Thou oft makest light of promise thou hast made.
Had I known the ennui is so hard to elude,
I would then have thee stayed.
What I can't bear to think, thy gallantry apart,
Is something else in thee that captivates my heart.
If one day I don't think of it,
A thousand times my brows will knit.


**Tune: "Bells Ringing in the Rain"**

Cicadas chill
Drearily shrill.
We stand face to face at an evening hour
Before the pavilion, after a sudden shower.
Can we care for drinking before we part?
At the city gate
We are lingering late,
But the boat is waiting for you to depart.
Hand in hand, we gaze at each other's tearful eyes
And burst into sobs with words congealed on our lips.
You'll go your way
Far, far away
On miles and miles of misty waves where sail the ships
And evening clouds hang low in boundless southern
    skies.

Lovers would grieve at parting as of old.
How could you stand this clear autumn day so cold!

Where will you be found at daybreak
From wine awake?
Moored by a riverbank planted with willow trees
Beneath the waning moon and in the morning breeze.
You'll be gone for a year.
What could I do with all bright days and fine scenes
    here!
Howe'er coquettish I am on my part,
To whom can I lay bare my heart?


**Tune: "Eight Beats of Ganzhou Song"**

Shower by shower
The evening rain besprinkles the sky
Over the river,
Washing cool the autumn air both far and nigh.
Gradually frost falls and blows the wind so chill
That few people pass by the hill or rill.
In fading sunlight drowned is my bower.
Everywhere the red and the green wither away,
There's no more splendour of a sunny day.
Only the waves of River Long
Silently eastward flow along.

I cannot bear
To climb high and look far, for to gaze where
My native land is lost in mists so thick
Would make my lonely heart homesick.
I sigh to see my rovings year by year.
Why should I linger hopelessly now there, now here?
From her bower my lady fair
Must gaze with longing eye.
How oft has she mistaken homebound sails
On the horizon for mine?
How could she know that I,
Leaning upon the rails,
With sorrow frozen on my face, for her do pine!

## Tune: "Imperial Capital Recalled"

In thin quilt on small pillow when weather is cold,
I begin to feel now the parting sorrow deep.
I toss from side to side until night has grown old;
I get up and lie down, but I can't fall asleep.
The night seems to appear
As long as a whole year.

I want to go back to see you and stay,
But I'm already far away.
Thousands of thoughts and lame excuses only
Make me feel all the more weary and lonely.
I shall miss you for the rest of my years,
Which can't compensate you for all your tears.


## *FAN ZHONG-YAN (989-1052)*


## Tune: "Screened by Southern Curtain"

Emerald clouds above
And yellow leaves below,
O'er autumn-tinted waves, cold, green mists grow.
The sun slants o'er the hills; the sky and waves seem
   one;
Unfeeling grass grows sweet beyond the setting sun.

A homesick heart
Lost in thoughts deep,
Only sweet dreams each night can retain me in sleep.
Don't lean alone on rails when the bright moon appears!
Wine in sad bowels would turn into nostalgic tears.

## ZHANG XIAN (990-1078)

### Tune: "Song of the Immortal"

Wine cup in hand, I listen to "The Water Song,"
Awake from wine at noon but not from sorrow long.
When will spring come back now it is going away?
In the mirror, alas!
I see happy time pass.
In vain may I recall the old days gone for aye.

Night falls on poolside sand where pairs of lovebirds
    stay;
The moon breaks through the clouds; with shadows
    flowers play.
Lamplight is veiled by screen on screen;
The fickle wind still blows,
The night quite silent grows.
Tomorrow fallen blooms on the way will be seen.

## YAN SHU (991-1055)

### Tune: "Silk-Washing Stream"*

I compose a new song and drink a cup of wine
In the bower of last year when weather is as fine.
When will you come back like the sun on the decline?

Deeply I sigh for faded flowers' fall in vain;
Vaguely I seem to know the swallows come again.
Loitering on the garden path, I alone remain.

---

* Written for a singing girl.

# ZHANG BIAN (992-1077)

## Tune: "Swallows Leaving Pavilion"

So picturesque the land by riverside,
In autumn tints the scenery is purified.
Without a break green waves merge into azure sky;
The sunbeams after rain take chilly dye.
Bamboo fence dimly seen on islets 'mid the reeds
And thatched cottages on the shore o'ergrown with
    weeds.

Among white clouds are lost white sails,
And where smoke coils up slow,
There wineshop flag hangs low.
How many of the fisherman's and woodman's tales
Are told about the Six Dynasties' fall and rise!*
Saddened, I lean upon the tower's rails;
Mutely the sun turns cold and sinks in western skies.

# SONG QI (998-1061)

## Tune: "Lily Magnolia Flowers"

The scenery is getting fine east of the town;
The rippling water greets boats rowing up and down.
Beyond green willows morning chill is growing mild;
On pink apricot branches spring is running wild.

In our floating life scarce are pleasures we seek after.
How can we value gold above hearty laughter?
I raise wine cup to ask the slanting sun to stay
And leave among the flowers its departing ray.

---

* Written at Jinling, capital of the Six Dynasties (221-280;
317-589).

## OUYANG XIU (1007-1072)

**Tune: "Treading on Grass"**

Roadside mume blossoms fade,
Riverside willows green,
On fragrant grass in the warm air a rider's seen.
The farther he goes, the longer his parting grief grows;
Endless like water in vernal river it flows.

With broken, tender heart
And tearful, longing eye,
His wife won't lean on railings of the tower high.
Beyond the far-flung plain mountains shut out her view;
The rider's farther away than the mountains blue.

**Tune: "Butterflies Lingering Over Flowers"**

Deep, deep the courtyard where he is, so deep
It's veiled by smokelike willows heap on heap,
By curtain on curtain and screen on screen.
Leaving his saddle and bridle, there he has been
Merrymaking. From my tower his trace can't be seen.

The third moon now, the wind and rain are raging late;
At dusk I bar the gate,
But I can't bar in spring.
My tearful eyes ask flowers, but they fail to bring
An answer; I see red blossoms fly o'er the swing.

## ZHENG GONG (1019-1083)

### The West Tower

The billows come and go like cloud;
The north wind blows up thunder loud.
All curtains rolled up in west tower;
From hill on hill comes sudden shower.

## SIMA GUANG (1019-1086)

### Tune: "The Moon Over the West River"

Loosely she has done up her hair;
Thinly she has powdered her face.
In rosy smoke and purple mist she looks so fair;
As light as willow down she walks with grace.

Before we part, we long to meet;
Amorous, she seems not in love.
Awake from wine and songs so sweet,
She finds the courtyard still and bright the moon above.

## WANG AN-SHI (1021-1086)

### Tune: "Fragrance of Laurel Branch"

I climb a height
And strain my sight;
Of autumn late it is the coldest time;
The ancient capital looks sublime.
The limpid river, beltlike, flows a thousand miles;
Emerald peak on peak towers in piles.
In the declining sun sails come and go;

In the west wind wineshop flags flutter high and low.
The painted boat
In clouds afloat,
Like stars in Silver River* egrets fly.
What a picture before the eye!

The days gone by
Saw people in opulence vie.
Alas! Shame came on shame under the walls,**
In palace halls.
Leaning on rails, in vain I utter sighs
O'er ancient kingdoms' fall and rise.
The running water saw the Six Dynasties pass,
But I see only chilly mist and withered grass.
E'en now the songstresses still sing
The songs composed by captive king.

**Tune: "Song of the Southern Country"**

The capital was ruled by kings since days gone by.
The rich green and lush gloom breathe a majestic sigh.
Like dreams has passed the reign of four hundred long
　　years,
Which calls forth tears.
Modern laureates are buried like their ancient peers.

Along the river I go where I will,
Up city walls and watch towers I gaze my fill.
Do not ask what has passed without leaving a trail!
To what avail?
The endless river rolls in vain beyond the rail.

---

　* The Chinese name for the Milky Way.
　** Rulers capitulated under the walls of their capital during the
Six Dynasties (221-280; 317-589).

# WANG AN-GUO (1028-1074)

### Tune: "Shortened Form of Lily Magnolia Flowers"

'Neath painted bridge water flows by;
The fallen flowers wet with rain can no more fly.
The moon breaks through twilight;
Fragrance within the curtain's smelt ere I alight.

Silently lingering around,
Where will my dreaming soul tonight be found?
Unlike the weeping willow,
Whose down will fly into your room and on your pillow.

# YAN JI-DAO (1030-1106)

### Tune: "Immortal at the River"

Awake from dreams, I find the locked tower high;
Sobered from wine, I see the curtain hanging low.
As last year spring grief seems to grow;
Amid the falling blooms alone stand I;
In the fine rain a pair of swallows fly.

I still remember when I first saw pretty Ping*
In silken dress embroidered with two hearts in a ring,
Revealing lovesickness by touching pipa's string.
The moon shines bright just as last year;
It did see her like a cloud disappear.

---

* A lutanist, or pipa player.

**Tune: "Partridge Sky"**

Time and again with coloured sleeves you tried to fill
My cup with wine that, drunk, I kept on drinking still.
You danced until the moon hung low o'er willow trees;
You sang until amid peach blossoms blushed the breeze.

Then came the time to part,
But you're deep in my heart.
How many times have I met you in dreams at night!
Now left to gaze at you in silver candlelight,
I fear it is not you
But a sweet dream untrue.


## *CHENG HAO (1032-1085)*

**Impromptu Lines on a Spring Day**

Towards noon 'neath fleecy clouds and gentle breeze
I cross the stream 'mid blooms and willow trees.
Some worldlings who don't know my heart's deep
　　pleasure
Would say I'm like a truant fond of leisure.


## *WANG GUAN (fl. 1057)*

**Tune: "Song of Divination"**

A stretch of rippling water is a beaming eye;
The arched brows around are mountains high.
If you ask where the wayfarer is bound,
Just see where beaming eyes and arched brows are
　　found.

I've just seen spring depart,
And now with you I'll part.
If you o'ertake in the south the spring day,
Oh! Be sure not to let it slip away!


# SU SHI (1037-1101)


## Drinking at the Lake, First in Sunny, Then in Rainy Weather

The brimming waves delight the eye on sunny days;
The dimming hills present rare view in rainy haze.
West Lake may be compared to Beauty of the West;*
It becomes her to be adorned or plainly drest.


## Tune: "Spring in the Garden of Qin"

*Written to my brother on my way to Mizhou.***

The lamp burns with green flames in an inn's lonely
    hall;
Wayfarers' dreams are broken by the cock's loud call.
Slowly the blooming moon rolls up her silk dress white;
The frost begins to shimmer in the soft daylight;
The cloud-crowned hills outspread their rich brocade
And morning dewdrops gleam like pearls displayed.
As the way of the world is long,
But toilsome life is short,
So, for a man like me, joyless is oft my sort.
After humming this song,
Silent, on my saddle I lean,
Brooding over the past, scene after scene.

---

* Xi Shi (fl. 482 B.C.), a beautiful lady born near West Lake.
** Mizhou was a poor district where officials under a cloud were
sent.

Together to the capital we came,
Like the two brothers Lu of literary fame.
A fluent pen combined
With a widely read mind,
Why could we not have helped the crown
To attain great renown?
As times require,
We advance or retire;
With folded arms we may stand by.
If we keep fit,
We may enjoy life before we lose it.
So drink the wine cup dry!


**Tune: "A Riverside Town"**

*Dreaming of my deceased wife on the night of the twentieth day of the first moon.\**


For ten long years the living of the dead knows nought.
Though to my mind not brought,
Could the dead be forgot?
Her lonely grave is far, a thousand miles away.
To whom can I my grief convey?
Revived, e'en if she be, oh, could she still know me?
My face is worn with care
And frosted is my hair.

Last night I dreamed of coming to our native place;
She's making up her face
Before her mirror with grace.
Each saw the other hushed,
But from our eyes tears gushed.
When I am woken, oh, I know I'll be heartbroken
Each night when the moon shines
O'er her grave clad with pines.

---

\* In 1075 the poet dreamed of his first wife, Wang Fu, whom he married in 1054 and who died in 1065.

## Tune: "Prelude to Water Melody"

*On the night of the Mid-autumn Festival of 1076 I drank happily till dawn and wrote this in my cups while thinking of my brother.*

How long will the full moon appear?
Wine cup in hand, I ask the sky.
I do not know what time of year
'Twould be tonight in the palace on high.
Riding the wind, there I would fly,
Yet I'm afraid the crystalline palace would be
Too high and cold for me.
I rise and dance; with my shadow I play.
On high as on earth, would it be as gay?

The moon goes round the mansions red
Through gauze-draped windows soft to shed
Her light upon the sleepless bed.
Against man she should have no spite.
Why, then, when people part, is she oft full and bright?
Men have sorrow and joy; they part or meet again;
The moon is bright or dim and she may wax or wane.
There has been nothing perfect since the olden days.
So let us wish that man
Will live long as he can!
Though miles apart, we'll share the beauty she displays.

## The Hundred-Pace Rapids

*When Wang Ding-guo was visiting me at Pengcheng (Xuzhou), he went one day with Yan Fu in a small boat, accompanied by three singing girls, for an outing on the River Si. To the north they climbed Holy Woman Hill; southward they poled down the Hundred-Pace Rapids, playing flutes, drinking wine, and returning home by moonlight. I had business to attend to and could not go*

*with them, but when evening came and I had changed
into informal Taoist robes, I stood at the top of the
Yellow Tower and gazed in the direction they had gone,
laughing and thinking to myself that not since the poet
Li Bai had died some three hundred years ago had
there been such a merry expedition. Wang Ding-guo
went away, and the following month Abbot Can-liao
and I poled down those same rapids, thinking of that
earlier outing, which now seemed like an event of the
distant past. Sighing to myself, I composed these two
poems. One I gave to Abbot Can-liao, the other I sent
to Wang Ding-guo.\**

Waves leap up where the long, long rapids steeply fall;
A light boat southward shoots like plunging shuttle, lo!
Water birds fly up at the boatman's desperate call.
Among the rocks it strives to thread its way and go
As a hare darts away, an eagle dives below,
A gallant steed runs down a slope beyond control,
A string snaps from a lute, an arrow from a bow,
Lightning cleaves clouds or off lotus leaves raindrops
     roll.
The mountains whirl around, the wind sweeps by the
     ear,
I see the current boil in a thousand whirlpools.
At the risk of my life I feel a joy without peer,
Just like the god who boasts of the river he rules.
Our life will pass like water running day and night;
Our thoughts can in a twinkling go beyond ninth sphere.
Many people in drunken dreams contend and fight.
Do they know palaces 'mid weeds will disappear?
Awakened, they'd regret they've lost a thousand days;
Coming here, they will find the river freely rolls.
If on the riverside rocks you turn your gaze,
You will find only honeycombs of the punt poles.
If your mind from earthly things is detached and freed,
Although nature may change, at ease you will remain.

---

\* Not selected in this anthology.

Let us go back in a boat or on a steed.
Our Abbot will not like such an argument vain.

### Tune: "Joy of Eternal Union"

*I lodged at the Pavilion of Swallows in Pencheng,
dreamed of the fair lady Pan-pan and wrote the
following lyric.*

The bright moonlight is like frost white,
The breeze is cool like waves serene;
Far and wide extends the night scene.
In the haven fish leap
And dewdrops roll down lotus leaves
In solitude no man perceives.
Drums beat thrice in the night so deep,
E'en a leaf falls with sound so loud
That, gloomy, I awake from my dream of the cloud.
Under the boundless pall of night,
Nowhere again can she be found,
Although I've searched o'er the garden's ground.

A tired wanderer far from home
Vainly through mountains and hills may roam;
His native land from view is blocked.
The Pavilion of Swallows is empty. Where
Is the lady Pan-pan so fair?
In the pavilion only swallows' nest is locked.
Both the past and the present are like dreams
From which we have ne'er been awake, it seems.
We've left but pleasures old and sorrows new.
Some future day others will come to view
The Yellow Tower's night scenery;
Would they then sigh for me!

## Tune: "Song of a Fairy in the Cave"

*When I was seven, a ninety-year-old nun told me that she had visited the palace of King Meng Chang, where she saw, on a sweltering hot night, the king and his favourite, Lady Pistil\*, sitting in the shade by a big pool, writing a poem, which she could still recite. Now forty years have passed. As the nun died long ago, nobody knows that poem now. I still remember the first two lines and think it was perhaps written to the tune of the "Song of a Fairy in the Cave." So I complete Meng Chang's poem as follows:*

Your jadelike bones and icelike skin
Are naturally sweatless, fresh and cool.
The breeze brings unperceivable fragrance in
And fills the bower by the pool.
The broidered screen rolled up lets in
The moon, which peeps at you so fair,
Leaning upon the pillow, not asleep, a pin
Across dishevelled hair.

We two rise hand in hand;
Silent in the courtyard we stand.
At times we see shooting stars stray
Across the Milky Way.
How old has night become?
The watchmen thrice have beaten the drum.
The golden moonbeams fade,
Low is the Dipper's string of jade.
We count on fingers when the western wind will blow.
What can we do with years that drift as rivers flow?

---

\* See Lady Pistil's poem, "Written at the Capitulation of the Kingdom of Shu."

## Tune: "Charm of a Maiden Singer"
## Memories of the Past at Red Cliff*

The endless river eastward flows;
With its huge waves are gone all those
Gallant heroes of bygone years.
West of the ancient fortress appears
Red Cliff, where General Zhou Yu won his early fame
When the Three Kingdoms were in flame.
Jagged rocks tower in the air
And swashing waves beat on the shore,
Rolling up a thousand heaps of snow.
To match the hills and the river so fair,
How many heroes brave of yore
Made a great show!

I fancy General Zhou Yu at the height
Of his success, with a plume fan in hand,
In a silk hood, so brave and bright,
Laughing and jesting with his bride so fair,
While enemy ships were destroyed as planned
Like castles in the air.
Should their souls revisit this land,
Sentimental, his bride would laugh to say:
Younger than they, I have my hair turned grey.
Life is like a passing dream.
O moon, I drink to you who saw them on the stream.

## Written on the Wall of West Forest Temple**

It's a range viewed in face and peaks viewed from the
    side,
Assuming different shapes viewed from far and wide.
Of Mount Lu we cannot make out the true face,
For we are lost in the heart of the very place.

---

\* Scene of the battle in A.D. 208 when General Zhou Yu defeated
Cao Cao's advancing forces.
\*\* Written when the poet visited Mount Lu in Jiangxi Province.

## Tune: "Water-dragon Chant"

*After Zhang Zhi-fu's lyric on willow catkins, using the
same rhyme scheme.*

They seem to be but are not flowers;
None pity them when they fall down in showers.
Forsaking leafy home,
By the roadside they roam.
I think they're fickle, but they've sorrow deep.
Their grief-o'erladen bowels tender,
Like willow branches slender.
And willow leaves like wistful eyes near shut with sleep,
About to open, yet soon closed again.
They dream of drifting with the wind for long,
Long miles to find their men,
But are aroused by orioles' song.

Grieve not for willow catkins flown away,
But that in Western Garden fallen petals red
Can't be restored. When dawns the day
And rain is o'er, we cannot find their traces
But in a pond with duckweeds overspread.*
Of spring's three graces,
Two have gone with the roadside dust
And one with waves. But if you just
Take a close look, then you will never
Find willow down but tears of those who sever,
Which drop by drop
Fall without stop.

---

* The poet's own note: It is said that when willow down falls into
the water, it turns into duckweed.

# LI ZHI-YI (1038-1117)

**Tune: "Song of Divination"**

I live upstream and you downstream;
From night to night of you I dream.
Unlike the stream, you're not in view,
Though both we drink from River Blue.

When will the river no more flow?
When will my grief no longer grow?
I wish your heart would be like mine,
Then not in vain for you I'd pine.

# HUANG TING-JIAN (1045-1105)

**Tune: "Pure, Serene Music" Late Spring**

Away spring goes!
Which way, which way?*
Whoever knows,
Please call her back to stay!

Spring's gone. Towards which land?
Ask orioles, who sing
A hundred tunes none understand.
Riding the wind, they're on the wing.

---

* This and the following line, Weng Xian-liang's translation versified.

## QIN GUAN (1049-1100)

### Tune: "Courtyard Full of Fragrance"

A belt of clouds girds mountains high
And withered grass spreads to the sky;
The painted horn at the watchtower blows.
Before my boat sails up,
Let's drink a farewell cup.
How many things do I recall in bygone days
All lost in mist and haze!
Beyond the setting sun I see but dots of crows
And that around a lonely village water flows.

I'd call to mind the soul-consuming hour
When I took off your perfume purse unseen
And loosened your silk girdle in your bower.
All this has merely won me in the mansion green*
The name of fickle lover.
Now I'm a rover,
Oh, when can I see you again?
My tears are shed in vain;
In vain they wet my sleeves.
It grieves
My heart to find your bower out of sight;
It's lost at dusk in city light.

### Tune: "Immortal at the Magpie Bridge"

Clouds float like works of art;
Stars shoot with grief at heart.
Across the Milky Way the Cowherd meets the Maid.**

---

* The mansion where beautiful singing girls lived.
** According to Chinese legend, the Cowherd and the Maid, or
the Weaver, two stars separated by the Milky Way, were to meet
across a magpie bridge once every year on the seventh day of the
seventh lunar month.

When autumn's Golden Wind embraces Dew of Jade,
All the love scenes on earth, however many, fade.

Their tender love flows like a stream;
This happy date seems but a dream.
How can they bear a separate homeward way?
If love between both sides can last for aye,
Why need they stay together night and day?

## Tune: "A Riverside Town"

Like northbound swan and southward-flying swallow
    fleet,
By chance we meet;
Sadly we greet.
We see no more dark hair and beaming face of then
But two old feeble men.
Don't ask about the long, long years since we did part!
Whatever wrings the heart,
Better keep it apart!

Draw from this vat rice wine we made in spring,*
Every drop glistening.
There is no hurry. Fill our golden cup!
Having drunk up,
Like flowers fallen on the stream we go our way.
We'll meet someday,
But who knows where? The misty waves stretch far and
    nigh,
Cloudy the evening sky.

---

* Weng Xian-liang's translation versified.

## HE ZHU (1052-1125)

**Tune: "The Partridge Sky"**

All things have changed. Once more I pass the city gate.
We came together; I go back without my mate.
Bitten by hoary frost, half of the plane tree dies;
Lifelong companion lost, one lonely lovebird flies.

Grass wet with dew
Dries on the plain;
How can I leave our old abode and her grave new!
In a half-empty bed I hear the pelting rain.
Who will turn up the wick to mend my coat again?

**Tune: "Green-Jade Cup"**

Never, never again
Will you tread on the waves along the lakeside lane!*
I follow with my eyes
The fragrant dusts that rise.
With whom are you now spending your delightful
    hours,
Playing on zither string,
On a bridge 'neath the moon, in a yard full of flowers,
Or at the curtained window of a crimson bower,
A dwelling only known to spring?

At dusk the floating cloud leaves the grass-fragrant
    plain;
With blooming brush I write heartbroken verse again.
If you ask me how deep and wide I am lovesick,
Just see the misty stream where weed grows thick,
The town o'erflowed with willow down that wafts on
    breeze,
The drizzling rain that yellows all mume trees!

---

* The poet lived on the lakeside lane.

# ZHOU BANG-YAN (1057-1121)

### Tune: "Auspicious-Dragon Chant"

Along the street to mansions green*
Some twigs of faded mumes can still be seen
And peach trees try to put forth blossoms sweet.
So quiet are the houses on the street;
The swallows seeking rest
Come back to their old nest.

I stand still, lost in thought of you,
So young, so fond, who came
To peep through cracks between the door and its frame.
At dawn, just thinly powdered in the yellow hue,
Against the wind you tried to hide
Your face in sleeves, giggling aside.

I who once came now come again;
Neighbouring houses still remain,
Where I saw you sing and dance then.
Only the Autumn Belle of yore
Enjoys a fair fame as before.

Trying my pen, I write a poem new.
Can I forget the old one writ for you?
If I but knew
Who is drinking with you in a garden of pleasure,
Or strolling now with you east of the town at leisure!
The past is gone
With lonely swan.
I seek for spring
Only to find past sorrow lingering.
The willows bend with their leaves painted gold;
I come away as it is late and cold.
The poolside drizzle grieves.
Back to the heartbreaking courtyard,

* The mansions where beautiful singing girls lived.

I see scenery willow down weaves
As wind blows hard.


## Tune: "Wandering of a Youth"*

Southern salt white as snow, northern knife bright as
    ice,
Her fingers fair a fresh mandarin orange slice.
In the just warmed-up curtained room they are
    sojourning;
In animal-shaped burner incense ne'er stops burning.
As they sit face to face,
She plays on flute with grace.

To him she whispers low,
"Where will you go?
The watchmen have already gone three rounds.
Horse hoofs may slip on frosty grounds.
You'd better stay.
There are few people on the way."


## MOQI YONG (fl. 1100-1125)


## Tune: "Everlasting Longing"

Watch after watch
And drop by drop,
The rain falls on banana leaves without a stop.
Within the window by the candlelight,
For you I'm longing all the night.

---

* The poet was once the rival of Emperor Hui Zong of the Song
Dynasty for the love of a famous singing girl, Li Shi-shi. One night
he was with her when the emperor came with a fresh mandarin
orange. The poet hid under the bed, heard what they said and wrote
this lyric.

I cannot seek for dreams
Nor banish sorrow.
The rain cares not what I dislike, it seems;
On marble steps it drips until the morrow.

## ZHU DUN-RU (1081-1159)

**Tune: "Joy at Meeting"**

I lean on western railings on the city wall
Of Jinling* in the fall.
Shedding its rays o'er miles and miles, the sun hangs low
To see the endless river flow.

The Central Plain is in a mess;
Officials scatter in distress.
When to recover our frontiers?
Ask the sad wind to blow over Yangzhou my tears!

## ZHAO JI (1082-1135)**

**Tune: "Hillside Pavilion" Apricot Seen in the North**

Petals on petals of well-cut fine silk ice-white,
Evenly touched with rouge light,
Your fashion new and overflowing charm make shy
All fragrant palace maids on high.
How easy 'tis for you to fade!
You cannot bear the cruel wind and shower's raid on
    raid.

---

* Jinling, present-day Nanjing, was on the southern shore of the
Yangtze River and Yangzhou on the northern shore, occupied by the
Jurchen invaders.
** Emperor Hui Zong of the Song Dynasty (see Zhou Bang-yan's
poem), captured by Jurchen invaders and sent to the north as
captive.

I'm sad to ask the courtyard sad and drear
How many waning springs have haunted here.

My heart is overladen with deep grief.
How could a pair of swallows give relief?
Could they know what I say?
'Neath boundless sky my ancient palace's far away.
Between us countless streams and mountains stand.
Could swallows find my native land?
Could I forget these mountains and these streams?
But I cannot go back except in dreams.
I know that dreams believed can never be,
But recently e'en dreams would no more come to me!


## LI QING-ZHAO (1084-1151)


**Tune: "Like a Dream"**

Last night the wind was strong and rain was fine;
Sound sleep did not dispel the taste of wine.
I ask the maid who's rolling up the screen.
"The same crab-apple tree," she says, "is seen."
"But don't you know,
But don't you know
The red should languish and the green must grow?"


**Tune: "A Twig of Mume Blossoms"**

Pink fragrant lotus fade; autumn chills mat of jade.
My silk robe doffed, I float
Alone in orchid boat.
Who in the cloud would bring me letters in brocade?
When swans come back in flight,
My bower's steeped in moonlight.

As fallen flowers drift and water runs their way,
One longing overflows
Two places with same woes.
Such sorrow can by no means be driven away;
From eyebrows kept apart,
Again it gnaws my heart.


## Tune: "Tipsy in the Flowers' Shade"

Thin is the mist and thick the clouds, so sad I stay.
From golden censer incense smokes all day.
The Double Ninth* comes now again;
Alone I still remain
In the curtain of gauze, on pillow smooth like jade,
Feeling the midnight chill invade.

At dusk I drink before chrysanthemums in bloom;
My sleeves are filled with fragrance and with gloom.
Say not my soul
Is not consumed. Should western wind uproll
The curtain of my bower,
'Twould show a thinner face than yellow flower.


## Tune: "Playing Flute Recalled on Phoenix Terrace"

Incense in gold
Censer is cold.
I toss in bed,
Quilt like waves red.
Getting up idly, I won't comb my hair;
My dressing table undusted, I leave it there.
Now the sun seems to hang on the drapery's hook.
I fear the parting grief would make me sadder look.
I've much to say, yet pause as soon as I begin.
Recently I've grown thin,

---

* On the ninth day of the ninth lunar month the poetess felt her
soul consumed by the separation from her dear husband.

Not that I'm sick with wine,
Nor that for autumn sad I pine.

Be done! Be done!
Once you are gone,
No matter what parting songs we sing anew,
We can't keep you.
Far, far away you pass your days;
My bower here is drowned in haze.
In front there is a running brook
That could never forget my longing look.
From now on, where
I gaze all day long with a vacant stare,
A new grief will grow there.


### Tune: "Spring in Peach-Blossom Land"

Sweet flowers fall to dust when winds abate.
Tired, I won't comb my hair although it's late.
Things are the same, but he's no more and all is o'er.
Before I speak, how can my tears not pour!

'Tis said at Twin Creek spring is not yet gone.
In a light boat I long to float thereon.
But I'm afraid the grief-o'erladen boat
Upon Twin Creek can't keep afloat.


### Tune: "Slow, Slow Song"

I look for what I miss;
I know not what it is.
I feel so sad, so drear,
So lonely, without cheer.
How hard is it
To keep me fit
In this lingering cold!
Hardly warmed up

By cup on cup
Of wine so dry,
Oh, how could I
Endure at dusk the drift
Of wind so swift?
It breaks my heart, alas,
To see the wild geese pass,
For they are my acquaintances of old.

The ground is covered with yellow flowers,
Faded and fallen in showers.
Who will pick them up now?
Sitting alone at the window, how
Could I but quicken
The pace of darkness that won't thicken?
On plane's broad leaves a fine rain drizzles
As twilight grizzles.
Oh, what can I do with a grief
Beyond belief!


## LU BEN-ZHONG (1084-1145)


**Tune: "Song of Picking Mulberries"**

I'm grieved to find you unlike the moon at its best,
North, south, east, west.
North, south, east, west,
It would accompany me without any rest.

I am grieved to find you like the moon, which would
    fain
Now wax now wane.
You wax and wane,
When will you come around like the full moon again?

## CHEN YU-YI (1090-1138)

**Tune: "Immortal at the River"**
**Mounting a Tower at Night and Recalling Old Friends**
**Visiting Luoyang Together**

I still remember drinking on the Bridge of Noon
With bright wits of the day.
The silent moon
On endless river rolled away.
In lacy shadows cast by apricot flowers
We played our flutes till morning hours.

O'er twenty years have passed like dreams;
It is a wonder that I'm still alive.
Carefree, I mount the tower bathed in moonbeams.
So many things passed long
Ago survive
Only in fishermen's midnight song.

## ZHANG YUAN-GAN (1091-1170)

**Tune: "Congratulations to the Bridegroom"**
**Seeing His Excellence Hu Quan\* Banished South**

Haunted by dreams of the lost Central Plain,
I hear the autumn wind complain.
From tent to tent horns dreary blow;
In ancient palace weeds o'ergrow.
How could Mount Pillar\*\* suddenly fall down
And Yellow River overflow the town,

---

    \* A high official of the Southern Song Dynasty who was against
the capitulatory policy and was banished in 1142 to the southernmost
place, where even wild geese carrying messages were not supposed to
go.
    \*\* Mount Pillar alludes to the royal court.

A thousand villages overrun with foxes and hares*?
We can't question the heaven high;**
The court will soon forget humiliating affairs.
'Tis sad and drear
To say good-bye
At Southern Pier.

Cold breath of river willows flies away
The remnant heat of summer day.
The Milky Way slants low;
Past pale moon and sparse stars clouds slowly go.
Mountains and rivers stretch out of view.
Oh, where shall I find you?
I still remember our talking at dead
Of night while we two lay in bed.
But now wild geese can't go so far.
Who will send my letters where you are?
I gaze on azure sky,
Thinking of the hard times gone by.
Can we have but personal love or hate
As beardless young men often state?
Hold up a cup of wine
And hear this song of mine!

## YUE FEI (1103-1141)

### Tune: "The River All Red"

Wrath sets on end my hair;
I lean on railings where
I see the drizzling rain has ceased.
Raising my eyes
Towards the skies,
I heave long sighs,

* Foxes and hares — the Jurchen aggressors.
** The heaven alludes to the emperor of the Song Dynasty.

My wrath not yet appeased.
To dust is gone the fame achieved in thirty years;
Like cloud-veiled moon the thousand-mile land
   disappears.*
Should youthful heads in vain turn grey,
We would regret for aye.

Lost our capitals,
What a burning shame!
How can we generals
Quench our vengeful flame!
Driving our chariots of war, we'd go
To break through our relentless foe.
Valiantly we'd cut off each head;
Laughing, we'd drink the blood they shed.
When we've reconquered our lost land,
In triumph would return our army grand.


## LU YOU (1125-1210)


### The Storm on the Fourth Day of the Eleventh Lunar Month

Forlorn in a cold bed, I'm grieved not for my plight,
Still thinking of recovering our lost frontiers.
Hearing the stormy wind and rain at dead of night,
I dreamed of frozen rivers crossed by cavaliers.

---

* The Central Plain was occupied by the Jurchen invaders.

## The Garden of Shen*

### (I)

Your fragrance has not sweetened my dreams for forty
    years;
The willows grow so old that no catkin appears.
I'll soon become a clod of clay beneath the hill;
Though drowned in tears, I come to find your traces
    still.

### (II)

The horn blows sad at sunset on the city wall;
In garden of old days I find no poolside hall.
To see green waves beneath the bridge would break my
    heart,
For they have seen your swanlike shadow come and
    part.

## Testament to My Son

After my death I know for me all hopes are vain,
But still I'm grieved to see our country not unite.
When royal armies recover the Central Plain,
Do not forget to tell your sire in sacred rite!

## Tune: "Phoenix Hairpin"***

Pink hands so fine,
Gold-branded wine,***

---

    * In the Garden of Shen the poet met his first wife, Tang Wan,
whom he loved dearly, yet was compelled to divorce. They wrote two
lyrics to the tune of "Phoenix Hairpin" in 1155. In 1200 the poet
revisited the garden alone and wrote these two poems.
    ** See Lu You's poem "The Garden of Shen."
    *** The wine offered to the poet by his first wife, Tang Wan.

Spring paints green willows palace walls cannot confine.
East wind unfair,
Happy times rare.
In my heart sad thoughts throng;
We've severed for years long.
Wrong, wrong, wrong!

Spring is as green,
In vain she's lean,
Her silk scarf soaked with tears and red with stains
    unclean.
Peach blossoms fall
Near deserted hall.
Our oath is still there. Lo!
No word to her can go.
No, no, no!

## TANG WAN (1128?-1156)

### Tune: "Phoenix Hairpin"*

The world unfair,
True manhood rare.
Dusk melts away in rain and blooming trees turn bare.
Morning wind high,
Tear traces dry.
I'll write to you what's in my heart,
Leaning on rails, speaking apart.
Hard, hard, hard!

Go each our ways!
Gone are our days.
Like long, long ropes of swing my sick soul groans
    always.
The horn blows cold,

---

* See Lu You's poem "The Garden of Shen."

Night has grown old.
Afraid my grief may be descried,
I try to hide my tears undried.
Hide, hide, hide!


## YANG WAN-LI (1127-1206)


### The West Lake

The uncommon West Lake in the midst of sixth moon
Displays a scenery to other months unknown:
Green lotus leaves outspread as far as boundless sky;
Pink lotus blossoms take from sunshine a new dye.


## ZHU XI (1130-1200)


### The Book*

There lies a glassy oblong pool,
Where light and shade pursue their course.
How can it be so clear and cool?
For water fresh comes from its source.


## ZHANG XIAO-XIANG (1132-1169)


### Tune: "The Charm of a Maiden Singer"
### Passing Lake Dongting

Lake Dongting, Lake Green Grass,
Near the Midautumn night,
Unruffled for no winds pass,

---

* The book is compared to a clear pool.

Like thirty thousand acres of jade bright
Dotted with the leaflike boat of mine.
The skies with pure moonbeams o'erflow;
The water surface paved with moonshine:
Brightness above, brightness below.
My heart with the moon becomes one,
Felicity to share with none.

Thinking of the southwest, where I passed a year,
To lonely pure moonlight akin,
I feel my heart and soul snow- and ice-clear.
Although my hair is short and sparse, my gown too thin,
In the immense expanse I keep floating up.
Drinking wine from the River West
And using Dipper as wine cup,
I invite Nature to be my guest.
Beating time aboard and crooning alone,
I sink deep into time and place unknown.

## XIN QI-JI (1140-1207)

**Tune: "Groping for Fish"**

*In 1179, before I was transferred from Hubei to Hunan,
Wang Zheng-zhi, a colleague of mine, feasted me in the
Little Hill Pavilion and I wrote the following.*

How much more can spring bear of wind and rain?
Too hastily 'twill leave again.
Lovers of spring would fear to see the flowers red
Budding too soon and fallen petals too widespread.
O spring, please stay!
I've heard it said that sweet grass far away
Would stop you from seeing your return way.
But I've not heard
Spring say a word;

Only the busy spiders weave
Webs all day by the painted eave
To keep the willow down from taking leave.

Could a disfavoured consort again to favour rise?
Could beauty not be envied by green eyes?
Even if favour could be bought back again,
To whom of this unanswered love can she complain?
Do not dance, then!
Have you not seen
Both plump and slender beauties turn to dust?
Bitterest grief is just
That you can't do
What you want to.
Oh, do not lean
On overhanging rails where the setting sun sees
Heartbroken willow trees!*


## Tune: "Slow Song of Zhu Ying-tai" Late Spring

E'er since we parted
At Ferry of Peach Leaf,
The willow-darkened southern bank's been drowned in
  grief.
I dread to go upstairs again;
Nine days in ten are filled with wind and rain.
So, brokenhearted,
I see red petals fall one by one,
Uncared for, and there's none
To plead with orioles singing all the day long
To still their song.

---

* In the first stanza the poet sighed for the departing spring, for
he and Wang could not do what they wanted, that is, drive away
Jurchen invaders from the occupied territory. In the second stanza
he compared Wang to a disfavoured beauty and the capitulators to
plump and slender dancers in favour. The willow trees were
heartbroken, for they saw the sun on the decline.

Peering at flowered hairpin on my head,
I take it down to count the petals red
So that I may anticipate
Your returning date,
Till lamplight flickers on my curtained bed.
Words choked in my dream upon
My lips: "Oh, grief has come with spring! I say,
Now spring is gone,
Why won't it carry grief away?"


**Tune: "Congratulations to the Bridegroom"**
**We Are Few***

That I should have aged so!
And my fellows, alas! How many still remain?
Life spent with naught to show
But hair turned silvery in vain.
Yet with a smile I part
With all that is mundane,
Whereof nothing gladdens the heart.
Charming are mountains green.
I would expect the feeling to be
Mutual, for we
Are somewhat alike, in mood and mien.

As I sit at the east window, goblet in hand,
My thoughts go to that poet of Peach-Blossom Land**
Who bemoaned scattered friends and louring cloud.
He was the philosophic drinker true,
Unlike those who
Of fickle fame felt proud.
I turn back crying;
An angry blast be raised and dark clouds flying!
It matters little I can't see the men of old;
Rather a pity they cannot see me!
But even my contemporaries, all told,

---

* Weng Xian-liang's translation versified.
** See Tao Qian's poem "Return to Nature."

How many of them really know me?
But two or three.


**Tune: "The Partridge Sky"**

*As a friend of mine talked about the victory we had won
while young, I recollected those bygone days and wrote
the following random lyric.*


While young, beneath my flag I had ten thousand
   knights;
With these outfitted cavaliers I crossed the river.
The foe prepared their silver shafts during the nights;
During the days we shot arrows from golden quiver.

Recalling days gone by,
I sigh over my plight;
The vernal wind can't change my hair to black from
   white.
Since thwarted is my plan for gaining the lost land,
I'd learn from neighbours how to plant fruit trees by
   hand.


**Tune: "Spring in Peach-Blossom Land"***
**Home Coming**

"Just a round trip of three hundred li.
Be back in five days," you told me.
Now I'm one day o'erdue,
Which must mean long hours of anxiety for you.

"Giddap!" My galloping horse seems too slow,
For impatient I grow.
I shout to a passing magpie,
"Go quick! Tell her I'm coming. Fly!"

---
* Weng Xian-liang's translation versified.

## CHEN LIANG (1143-1194)

**Tune: "Prelude to Water Melody" Farewell to Zhang
De-mao,\* Envoy to Jurchen Aggressors**

Not seeing southern troops for long,
Don't say their northern steeds can't run.
Single-handed, at once the thing is done;
After all, we are heroes millions strong.
His Majesty's envoy — what fun! —
Should eastward go like overbrimming river
That eastward flows forever.
We bend to the Jurchen tents now;
Another day to us they'll bow.

In the capital of our emperors
And the land of great, long
Empire built by our ancestors,
Is there none who thinks it wrong
To submit to the foe
Whose stink of mutton spreads for miles and miles?
Where's the spirit of heroes who died long ago?
When will our army beat the Jurchen ranks and files?
Why ask about the enemy's fate?
The sun\*\* will surely radiate.

---

\* Zhang De-mao was the envoy of the southern court, sent alone
to bow to the Jurchen chieftain, who was accustomed to eating
mutton.
\*\* The Song Empire.

# LIU GUO (1154-1206)

## Tune: "The Moon Over the West River"*

Ministers in the court plan the campaign;
Generals, spear in hand, guard the frontier.
When can we take back the lost Central Plain?
Our men, united, should start now and here.

Holding the premiership today,
You'll win high honour tomorrow.
The capital retaken, you may sing the lay
Of "Big Wind"** and people will follow.

# JIANG KUI (1155-1221)

## Tune: "The Partridge Sky" A Dream
## on the Night of Lantern Festival***

The endless River Fei to the east keeps on flowing;
The love seed we once sowed forever keeps on growing.
Your face I saw in dream was not clear to my eyes
As in your portrait; soon I'm awakened by birds' cries.

Spring not yet green,
My grey hair seen,
Our separation's been too long to grieve the heart.
Why make the past reappear
Before us from year to year
On Lantern Festival when we are far apart?

---

 * This lyric was written for Premier Han, who planned a northern
campaign to take back the lost Central Plain and the lost capital.
 ** See Liu Bang's "Song of the Big Wind."
 *** On the fifteenth day of the first lunar month in 1197 the
over-forty-year-old poet dreamed of his beloved, from whom he had
been separated for over twenty years.

## *YE SHAO-WENG (fl. 1224)*

### Calling on a Friend Without Meeting Him

How could the green moss like the sabots, whose teeth*
  sting?
I tap long at the door, but none opens at my call.
The garden can't confine the full beauty of spring;
An apricot extends a blooming branch o'er the wall.


## *SHI DA-ZU (1163-1220)*

### Tune: "A Pair of Swallows"

Spring's growing old.
Between the curtain and the screen
The dust in last year's nest is cold.
A pair of swallows bank and halt to see
If they can perch there side by side.
Looking at painted ceiling and carved beams
And twittering, they can't decide,
It seems.
Clipping the tips of blooming tree,
They shed
The shadow of their forked tails so green
And cleave their way through flowers red.

Along the fragrant way
Where rain has wetted clods of clay
They like to skim over the ground,
Striving to be fleet
In flight.
Returning late to mansion sweet,
They've gazed their fill, till in twilight

* Chinese sabots had teeth.

Dim willows are drowned
And flowers fall asleep.
Now they'd be perching deep
In fragrant nest,
Forgetting to bring message from the end of sky.
Grieved, with eyebrows knit, the lady's seen to rest
Her elbow on the painted rails and sigh.


## LIU KE-ZHUANG (1187-1269)


**Tune: "Spring in the Garden of Qin"**
**Dreaming of a Deceased Friend***

Again we meet
In wineshop of the north**
And in Bronze Bird Tower. Let the cook make
    mincemeat
Of the whale caught in eastern sea
And stablemen bring forth
The fiery western steeds for you and me.
Heroes there are in this world: you and I.
Who deserves drinking in our company?
But I will call
Warriors and swordsmen who are not afraid to die.

Let the drums roll! And drink, drink deep!
But down to earth again. The cock wakes me from sleep.
So it's not to be, after all.
Great deeds might have been, had chance come my way.
It's too late now, I've lost my day.
Even a hero can win honours high
Only under a heroic sage.
Up! Let no future be o'ershadowed by
A nonheroic age!

---

* Weng Xian-liang's translation versified.
** The north was occupied by Jurchen invaders.

## WU WEN-YING (1200-1260)

### Tune: "Wind Through Pines"

Hearing the wind and rain while mourning for the
    dead,*
Sadly I draft an elegy on flowers.
We parted on the dark-green road before these bowers,
Where willow branches hang like thread,
Each inch revealing
Our tender feeling.
I drown my grief in wine in chilly spring;
Drowsy, I wake again when orioles sing.

In Garden West I sweep the pathway
From day to day,
Enjoying the fine view
Still without you.
On the ropes of the swing the wasps often alight
For fragrance spread by fingers fair.
I'm grieved not to see your foot traces; all night
The mossy steps are left untrodden there.

## LIU CHEN-WENG (1231-1294)

### Tune: "Green Tip of Willow Branch"

Tatar steeds in blankets clad,
Tears shed from lanterns** 'neath the moon,
Spring has come to a town so sad.
The flutes playing a foreign tune

---

  * Chinese people mourned for the dead on the eighth day of the
third lunar month.
  ** Lantern Festival in Lin'an (present-day Hangzhou), capital of
the Southern Song, occupied by the Tatars in 1276.

And foreign drumbeats in the street
Can never be called music sweet.

How can I bear to sit alone by dim lamplight,
Thinking of northern land now lost to sight
With palaces steeped in moonlight,
Of southern capital in days gone by,
Of my secluded life in mountains high,
Of grief of those who seaward fly*!

## WEN TIAN-XIANG** (1236-1282)

### Sailing on Lonely Ocean

Delving in the *Book of Change*, I rose through hardships
    great
And desperately fought the foe for four long years.
Like willow down the war-torn land looks desolate;
I sink or swim as duckweed in the rain appears.
For perils on Perilous Beach I heaved sighs;
On Lonely Ocean now I feel dreary and lonely.
Since olden days there's never been a man but dies;
I'd leave a loyalist's name in history only.

---

* The remnants of unyielding Song forces still carrying on armed
resistance on the sea.
** Wen Tian-xiang passed the civil service examinations with
highest honours in 1256 and was appointed prime minister in the
court of the Song Dynasty. In 1275 he led the royalist army against
the Tatar invaders. Defeated, he passed Perilous Beach in 1276.
Captured in 1278, he passed Lonely Ocean, a part of the South China
Sea.

## JIANG JIE (fl. 1274)

### Tune: "A Twig of Mume Blossoms"

Can boundless vernal grief be drowned in vernal wine?
On waves is tossed my boat;
Before wineshop flags float.
The farewell ferry and the bridge again I pass
When sadly blows the breeze
And rain falls without cease.

When may I go home to wash this outworn robe of mine,
To play on silver flute
And burn the incense mute?
Time and tide will never wait for man, alas!
Cherries red are seen
And bananas green.

## ZHANG YAN (1248-1320)

### Tune: "Ganzhou"

*In 1291 Sheng Yao-dao and I came back from the
north and then we went separately to Yuezhou and
Hangzhou. The next year he came to see me; we stayed
together for a few days and then parted again, so I
wrote the following song.*

I still remember at the Gate of Jade
A pleasure trip in snow was made.
Our sable coats were stiffened in cold air.
Treading on ancient road by forest bare
Or watering the steeds in endless stream,
We felt relieved as if past grief were but a dream.
But now awake, still on the southern shore I stand,

Shedding tears for my friend in western land.
No verse is written on the fallen leaf,
But still it feels unwritten grief.

You're carried back by a white cloud.
For whom should pendants tinkle loud?
Looking at shadows, who could still feel proud?
Breaking off flower reeds, I would send them afar,
But I'm saddened by autumn as they are.
As usual 'neath the bridge water runs by the shore,
But the gulls standing on the sand aren't those of yore.
In vain I sigh;
At sunset I'm afraid to climb up high.


## NIE SHENG-QIONG*


**Tune: "The Partridge Sky"****

I see you leave the town, jade-pale and sad like flower;
The willows look so green below the Lotus Tower.
Before a cup of wine I sing a farewell song;
At the fifth post I see you off on journey long.

I seek again
Sweet dreams in vain.
Who knows how deep is my sorrow?
My teardrops on the pillow
And raindrops on the willow
Drip within and without the window till the morrow.

---

* A singing girl in Chang'an (present-day Xi'an).
** The farewell song she sang to her beloved.

# YUAN DYNASTY
(1271-1368)

## *ZENG YONG-YUAN*

### Tune: "Rouged Lips"

The east wind blows all night;
My pillow laden with grief cannot be made light.
The cries of birds wake me from dreams;
I find my window bathed in sunny beams.

You came with spring
And go when spring is oldening.
The same green grass
Along the road beneath our feet
Only when you come back, alas,
Will become sweet.

## *MA ZHI-YUAN (1260-1334)*

### Tune: "Clear Sky Over the Sand" Autumn

O'er old trees wreathed with rotten vine fly evening
     crows;
'Neath tiny bridge beside a cot a clear stream flows;
On ancient road in western breeze a lean horse goes.
Westward declines the sun;
Far, far from home is the heartbroken one.

# GUAN HAN-QING (c.1220-c.1300)

### Tune: "Four Pieces of Jade" Separation

When you are gone,
For you I long.
When will my yearning come to an end?
I lean on rails, caressed by snowlike willow down.
The stream you went along
At hillside takes a bend.
It's screened from view,
Oh, together with you.

# WANG SHI-FU

### Tune: "Calm Dignity" Parting*

With clouds the sky turns grey
O'er yellow blooms-paved way.
How bitter blows the western breeze!
From north to south fly all wild geese.
Why like wine-flushed face is frosted forest red?
It's dyed in tears the parting lovers shed.

# ZHANG KE-JIU (1270-1349?)

### Tune: "Song of Clear River" Hermitage**

My sanctuary right in front of mountains proud.
The only intruder's the cloud.
How green the pines surging and singing in the breeze!

---

* From "Romance of the Western Chamber," IV, iii.
** Weng Xian-liang's translation versified.

How bright the tripod flames licking leaves of oak trees!
A jug of wine and then sleep still.
Oh, let spring go by as it will.


## QIAO JI (1280-1345)


### Tune: "Leaning on the Railings" on My Way to Jinglin*

On poetry-burdened jade far, far have I strayed.
The weary birds are wailing o'er huts on my way.
See how the willows shed their catkin at my head
As if it were not touched already with grey!

---

* Weng Xian-liang's translation versified.

# MING DYNASTY
(1368-1644)

## QI JI-GUANG* (1528-1587)

### March at Dawn

Our banners undulate along the winding stream
Without disturbing the riverside bird from its dream,
Suddenly we beat drums and blow our bugles shrill
Which startle even the deaf old monk beyond the hill.

## TANG XIAN-ZU

### From "The Peony Pavilion"

Ariot of deep purple and bright red.
What pity on the ruins they overspread!
Why does Heaven give us brilliant day and dazzling
    sight?
Whose house could boast of a sweeter delight?
At dawn on high rainbow clouds fly;
At dusk the green pavilion's seen.
In misty waves mingle the threads of rain;
The wind swells sails of painted boats in vain.
For those behind the screens
Make light of vernal scenes.

---

* A General and national hero in charge of national defence who
had won many victories against Japanese aggressors.

# QING DYNASTY
(1644-1911)

## *WU WEI-YE (1609-1671)*

### Song of the Beautiful Yuan-Yuan

The emperor left the human world on a gloomy day;
The general* to the imperial palace fought his way.
The royal armies dressed in mourning shed their tears;
The wrathful general for his lady wielded his spears.

"Not that I love my lady captured by the foe,
But that I hate to death the rebels spreading woe.
Like lightning sweeping them away at Mountain Black,
O'er father's death I'll weep and bring my lady back."

Remember their first meeting in a nobleman's bower:
She sang and danced as beautifully as a flower.
The nobleman promised to bestow the songstress fair
On General Wu, who carried her home in sedan chair.

Born near the Flower-Washing Stream, she was a maid
Named Yuan-yuan, whose charm outshone silk and
   brocade.
She dreamed of roving in the royal garden where
She met the king surrounded by his maidens fair.
In previous life he must have been the Fairy Queen;
Before her door there stretched a sea of water green.

---

\* General Wu, whose favourite lady Yuan Yuan was captured by
the peasant army, led the Qing forces in recapturing her in 1644
resulting in the downfall of the Ming Dynasty.

On water green two oars propelled a boat in flight:
A nobleman had carried her away by might.
Who knows on such occasion what her fate would be?
Her tear-soaked robe was all that one could see.

Her bitterness ascended to the skies.
But no one pitied her pearly teeth, her crystal eyes.
She was ravished and shut up inside all day long,
Where she was taught to sing every ravishing song.

The general came and drank his fill till sunset.
To whom could she complain and sing her deep regret?
With our young general bright no gallant could ever vie:
While plucking flowers sweet he often turned his eye.

He freed the singing bird caged behind stout bars.
How many times they crossed the Stream of Silver Stars!
But military orders commanded him to fight;
He promised to be back and left her in sad plight.

How deep his love for her! How hard again to meet
When rebels trampled the capital beneath their feet!
Alas! the lovesick mistress in the tower high
Was taken like the willow catkin in the sky.
Her inner chamber was surrounded all about;
From the carved balustrade she was compelled to come
    out.
Had not our general beaten the rebel force,
How could his lady fair be rescued on a horse?

The lady on a horse was summoned to appear,
Her hair like tousled cloud, unrecovered from fear.
Two giant candles lit her to the battlefield;
Her pretty face was clouded behind a veil of tears
    congealed.

The general's force, while beating drums, marched its
    way;
A thousand chariots drove southwest without delay.

In cloud-veiled valley rose a painted tower high;
The setting moon became a mirror to her eye.

To her homeland by riverside the news soon spread
Though ten times maples bitten by frost had turned red.
The master who taught her to sing felt fortunate;
The washerwomen still remembered their lucky mate.

"We're swallows pecking clods of clay to build our nest;
One flying up the tree becomes a phoenix blest.
Before a cup of wine we grieve that old we've grown;
We're glad she's married General Wu who wears a
    crown."

The lady then felt compromised by far-flung fame:
Her beauty earned for her all noblemen's acclaim.
One casket of bright pearls brought ten caskets of
    grief:
Her slender waist now wafted for miles like a leaf.
Blame not the breeze that blows down flowers far and
    nigh!
For boundless spring has come from the earth and sky.

A peerless beauty brings countries up and down
And earns for a gallant hero his lasting renown.
How could a woman care about the state affair?
How could our general forsake his lady fair?
His family slain and turned to dust and clay;
Her rosy dress will shine in history for aye.
Have you not seen
In Golden Palace where the lovebirds passed the night
The lady was too lovely to be kept out of sight?
On dusty fragrant path now only cries blackbird,
No beauty's steps are heard
Where moss in vain grows green.

Birds' feathers plucked and palace moved, for miles
    grief reigns:
Pearly teeth sing and green sleeves dance on western
    plains.

For the conquered Southern Land I sing another song;
But River Han still southeastward flows all day long.


## NALAN XINGDE (1655-1685)


### Tune: "Song of the Golden Thread" Rieve Not*

Why aggravate our misery?
Let gods do what they will.
Adamant we are; unsullied we shall be.
Life is less full of good than ill.
How many ancients did complain?
Justice is often denied to the intelligent.
Lying alone on a rude couch, I gaze at the Wain;
On city wall a flute is wailing a deep lament.
I hear the drum on the watchtower
Boom out the hour:
The darkest night
Is at its height.

Whoever would be a man
Should seek no patronage;
Better get ready a boat while we can
That we may on five lakes find anchorage.
Useless to staunch my tears copious as autumn rain.
Who would take notice but butterflies on the plain?
I do not envy those at court
Whose dizzy whirl is short.
I let the west wind blow
In capital and chill the moonlight waste!
The cloistered flowers are chaste
As virgin snow.

---

* Weng Xian-liang's translation versified.

## YUAN MEI (1716-1797)

### On Lady Yang*

Sing not of Lady Yang's regret of days gone by!
The Silver River severs on earth as on high.
In Stone Moat Village when the man parted from his
    wife,
More tears were shed than in the Palace of Long Life.

## CAO XUE-QIN (1715-1763)

### Lin Dai-yu's Elegy on Flowers

As flowers fall and fly across the skies,
Who rues the red that fades, the scent that dies?
Softly the gossamer floats over bowers green;
Gently the willow fluff wafts to broidered screen.

In my chamber I'm grieved to see spring depart.
Where can I pour out my sorrow-laden heart?
I step out of my portal with a hoe.
On fallen petals could I come and go?

Willow threads and elm leaves are fresh and gay;
They care not if peach and plum blossoms drift away.
The peach and plum will bloom next year.
But in my chamber who will then appear?

---

* Lady Yang (719-756) was the favourite mistress of Emperor
Xuan Zong of the Tang Dynasty. She lamented that they were
separated from each other in the Palace of Long Life just as the two
celestial lovers were separated by the Silver River (the Milky Way).
But they ignored the fact that their sufferings were nothing
compared with those they inflicted on their subjects (see Du Fu's
"Pressgang at Stone Moat Village").

By the third moon the swallows built their nest,
But apathetically on the beam they rest.
Next year though they may peck the buds again,
O in my empty chamber can their nest remain?

For three hundred and sixty days each year,
The cutting wind and biting frost make flowers sear.
How long can they blossom fresh and fair?
Once blown away, they cannot be found anywhere.

Their gravedigger, I find no flowers in bloom;
My aching heart is further filled with gloom.
With hoe in hand, tears secretly shed
Like drops of blood turn bare branches red.

At twilight falls, the cuckoos sing no more;
I come back with my hoe and close the door.
Abed in dim-lit room when night is still,
I hear cold rain and my quilt feels damp and chill.

I wonder why I'm thrown in such a fret:
Is it for love of spring or for regret?
I love it when it comes, regret it when it goes;
But spring comes and goes mute as water flows.

Last night from the courtyard a dirge was heard,
Sung by the soul of flower and of bird.
The bird's and flower's soul is hard to detain;
The flowers blush and silent birds remain.

I long on wings to fly
With flowers to the end of the earth and the sky.
At earth's uttermost bound,
Where can I find a fragrant burial mound?

Why don't I shroud in silken bag the petals fair
And bury them in the earth forever to mingle there?
Pure they come and pure shall go,
Not sinking to oblivion below.

Now they are dead, I come to bury them today.
Who can divine the date when I shall pass away?
Men laugh at my folly in burying fallen flowers.
But who will bury me when come my last hours?

See spring depart and flowers wither by and by.
This is the time when beauty must grow old and die.
Once spring is gone and beauty dead, alas!
Who will care for the fallen bloom and buried lass?